"Wow, this is some book,

I mean it's more than a beautiful and heavy trip, it's also very important in an evolutionary way, showing us directions we could be moving in—hopefully another sign that the Novel of Bullshit is dead and some kind of re-enlightenment is beginning to arrive, to take hold. Rudolph Wurlitzer is really, really good, and I hope he manages to come down again soon, long enough anyhow to guide us on another one like *Nog*." —Thomas Pynchon

"Rudolph Wurlitzer inhabits a nightmare world ... he renders his readers as breathless as himself ... an undeniable talent for those not subject to vertigo." —Alan Pryce-Jones
New York Post

"A genuine writing talent with an enormous lyrical quality." —Jacov Lind
author of *Landscape in Concrete*

"A strange, singular book.... Suggested for mature audiences." —*Newsweek*

NOG was originally published by Random House.

nog

by
Rudolph
Wurlitzer

PUBLISHED BY POCKET BOOKS NEW YORK

NOG

Random House edition published January, 1969
Pocket Book edition published January, 1970

This *Pocket Book* edition includes every word
contained in the original, higher-priced edition. It is printed
from brand-new plates made from completely reset, clear, easy-to-read
type. *Pocket Book* editions are published by Pocket Books, a division
of Simon & Schuster, Inc., 630 Fifth Avenue, New York, N.Y. 10020.
Trademarks registered in the United States and other countries.

Standard Book Number: 671–77143–4.
Library of Congress Catalog Card Number: 68–28552.
Copyright, ©, 1968, by Rudolph Wurlitzer. All rights reserved.
This *Pocket Book* edition is published by arrangement with Random
House.

Printed in the U.S.A.

nog

YESTERDAY afternoon a girl walked by the window and stopped for sea shells. I was wrenched out of two months of calm. Nothing more than that, certainly, nothing ecstatic or even interesting, but very silent and even, as those periods have become for me. I had been breathing in and out, out and in, calmly, grateful for once to do just that, staring at the waves plopping in, successful at thinking almost nothing, handling easily the three memories I have manufactured, when that girl stooped for sea shells. There was something about her large breasts under her faded blue tee shirt, the quick way she bent down, her firm legs in their rolled-up white jeans, her thin ankles—it was her feet, actually; they seemed for a brief, painful moment to be elegant. It was that thin-boned brittle movement with her feet that did it, that touched some spot that I had forgotten to smother. The way those thin feet remained planted, yet shifting slightly in the sand as she bent down quickly for a clam shell, sent my heart thumping, my mouth dry, no exaggeration, there was something gay and insane about that tiny gesture because it had nothing to do with her.

I went to Smitty's, a roadhouse a quarter of a mile down the beach. When I came back, she was gone. I could not sit in my room. The walls closed in on me. I could see the walls closing in on me, and my situation, if that is what it is, a situation, seemed suddenly so dull and hopeless; this cheap thrown-together guest house of imitation redwood on the California coast with its smell of mold and bad plumbing, the inane view from my window of driftwood and seaweed, flat predictable waves, corny writings in the sand, pot-bellied fishermen and bronzed godlike volleyball players. I had to pull out, I thought, I was beginning to notice things, lists were forming, comparisons were on the way. And now I don't have the octopus. I suppose that is what there is to tell about. Then I'll move on. Last night there was a storm, and I abandoned the octopus. I didn't really abandon the octopus, it's still in the bathysphere on the truck bed, and the truck bed is still up on blocks, but it's not the same any more. I'm going to move on alone.

I have money and I can make money. I want to say

that now. I'm no reprobate, nor am I a drain on anyone. My great aunt left me two thousand a year, and I have, or had, an octopus and a truck. A man sold me the octopus and truck in Oregon. I met him in a bar in one of those logging towns on the Coast where the only attractive spot is the village dump, which at least has the advantage of facing the sea. Nog, he was apparently of Finnish extraction, was one of those semi-religious lunatics you see wandering around the Sierras on bread and tea, or gulping down peyote in Nevada with the Indians. He was dressed in black motorcycle boots, jeans and an old army shirt with sergeant chevrons still on the sleeves. His face was lean and hatchet-edged, with huge fuzzy eyes sunk deep in his skull like bullet holes. He kept complaining about a yellow light that had lately been streaming out of his chest from a spot the size of a half dollar. We drank and talked about the spot and the small burning sensation it gave him early in the morning and about his octopus. He had become disillusioned about traveling with the octopus and had begun having aggressive dreams about it. He wanted to sell it. We bought a bottle and walked out beyond the town into logged-off hills that looked like old battlefields. A low mist hung over a struggling second growth of redwood and Douglas fir. The tracks of giant caterpillar tractors wound everywhere. Pits and ditches were scattered about like shell holes. Thousands of frogs croaked and salamanders hung suspended between lids of green slime and rotting logs. I felt vaguely elated, like a witness to some ancient slaughter.

Nog lived in what had once been a water tank in the

middle of a rough field. The octopus was there, all right. It was sitting inside a bathysphere on a truck bed. Nog had built a mold out of plaster of Paris for the tentacles and another one for the obese body with its parrot-like beak and bulging eyes. Then he had poured liquid latex rubber into the molds. The bathysphere was carefully fashioned out of a large butane gas tank and stolen pieces of metal from a nearby bridge. There were three portholes from which you could watch the octopus move its eight tentacles around in the bubbling water. Nog had been traveling to all the state and county fairs through the West and Midwest, charging kids a dime and adults a quarter. Most people believed the octopus was real, but whenever there was a loud doubt Nog would tell them the truth. He would never give money back, and occasionally there would be fights. In Bird City, Utah, the bathysphere had been tipped over by three men who had just been on a losing softball team. He was weary of the whole thing, he kept repeating. We sat down on a bench in front of his house, and he filled me in on octopus lore. The crowd appreciated the devilfish myth the most, and it was important to tell them how dangerous octopi are and how they can drown and mangle a human or sink a small boat. One should never tell them the truth, which is that octopi are quite friendly. I refused any more information. We sat quietly and it grew dark. Finally Nog said that he had stopped knowing how to entertain himself. He said he guessed that was my trouble, too, but that I should take a chance with the octopus. He suggested I transform it into a totem that I didn't mind seeing every day.

I bought the octopus, and for a year I traveled through the country with it.

Nog is not quite clear enough. I have to invent more. It always comes down to that. I never get a chance to rest. I have never been able, for instance, to understand the yellow light streaming from his chest. But now that the octopus has faded away, Nog might emerge into a clearer focus. Those were sentimental and fuzzy days, those trips through the West with the octopus, and sometimes I find myself wishing more of it were true. (I find, when I ruminate like this, that I invent a great deal of my memories—three now, to be exact—because otherwise I have trouble getting interested.) But I have gotten faster with myself and more even-tempered since I met Nog. Perhaps not even-tempered but certainly more dulcet. I think about trips, bits and pieces of trips, but I no longer try and put anything together (my mind has become blessedly slower), nor do I try as much to invent a suitable character who can handle the fragments. But I don't want to get into all that. There is always the danger that I might become impressed by what once was a misplaced decision for solitude.

I'm thinking about trying the East. I will go to New York and get a small room on the top of a hotel.

When I was on the road with the octopus I did a lot of reminiscing about New York. New York was, in fact, my favorite memory for four or five months, until it got out of hand and I had to drop it. I lived in a comfortable duplex apartment on top of an old hotel overlooking a small park and harbor. I was sort of an erotic spy on myself then, but managed to survive, at least for those four or five months, by keeping an alert and fastidious watch on the terrifying view outside. I watched ships glide and push into huge docks, and far below, through silvery leaves, the quiet violence in the park. At night I stayed up with the fantastic lights of cars and subways as they flowed over the concrete ramps that weaved around the hotel. I lived precariously in the center of brutal combinations of energy, and gradually, as I closed in on myself, the bridges transformed into massive spider webs imprisoning the subways as they rumbled like mechanical snakes across the black river. The subways shot off green and yellow sparks in defense, in specific relays of time, always getting through. I had to drop that memory. But now, with more miles and memories in control, I might attempt New York.

From my window I can see the beach. An old couple digs razorbacked clams, and a small boy writes "David Salte Hates the Slug" on the sand with a large knotted stick. It has never been enough for me to have a stick and some sand to draw in. I am not indifferent enough. I am too self-engrossed to play in the sand. But yesterday afternoon I was *trying* to at least get ready to play, trying to find the right approach, the right kind of silence, when the girl walked by. That touch of elegance ruined my confidence. It made me dwell on the time I have spent just getting by, made me hate the octopus and the kingdom of the octopus, the small towns, the long monotonous highways, the squalid fairgrounds. It made me take a walk on the beach.

It's a glorious beach, I suppose; usually empty, very

wide and sandy. In back there are warm and green mountains, and most of the time the sea is well behaved, although it was rough then and it had begun to rain. I began to think of beaches. I have been on eighty-seven beaches in the last fifteen years. Before that it is easier to be vague. Lately I have been reviewing each beach, although it isn't a satisfactory way of getting through the day. Too much of my life has been spent on beaches: Cannes, Far Rockaway, Stinson Beach, one beach in Ireland, two in Crete, Lido, Curaçao, Luquillo, Curadado, Malibu, Deya, Nice, Tangiers, Cob, the Virgin Islands—to name a few. I never run into the water. I am actually afraid of moving water. Nor do I get a suntan. I lie in one place, usually on my stomach, and do nothing. For me, beaches are profane.

So there I was, reaching the end of the beach, thinking about beaches, when I saw the girl again. She was standing near a black rock, a yellow shawl wrapped around her face, staring inanely at the sea. I walked up to her, and standing a little apart and to the rear of her, I too stared at the sea. The waves were rushing in and out, quite furious now, sucking at the stones. I looked at her. She seemed not to have noticed me, and for this I was grateful. I was happy enough just to stand there, next to her, for my former feelings about her foot were quite in control. In fact, I inspected her feet and it didn't seem possible that one of them should have acted as such a catalyst. Her feet were like her face, too broad and splotchy, rather crude and used up. Her dull features reassured me so much that I thought I might be able to stay on for another few months.

She turned towards me.

I have never been able to connect with strange women except if they are in distress or in some way hung up. She looked abysmally happy.

"You live in the boarding house, don't you?" she asked. "Yes, I think you're the only one who is permanent there."

I wasn't able to answer, a common fault of mine.

"What do you do? I mean, we've all been wondering what you do. You look frail and timid, like some great thinker or something. That's what I think, anyway. My husband thinks you're recovering from some romantic disease. Who's right, him or me?"

She sat down on the black rock. The rain was drenching us. I was unprepared for such a downpour, being dressed in white seersucker pants, white paisley shirt and finely-woven linen shoes. I stood near her, waiting, but resolved not to give out with any information. If pressed, I might improvise on one of my memories. One should have an electric mind, I decided right there, not a tepid half-awake coping mind.

"Walk me down the beach," the girl said. "I'm so wet. We're *both* so wet. You don't mind, do you? I'll tell you a secret, we call you Dr. Angst because of the gloom on your face. You don't mind, do you?"

I walked with her. I was, in fact, deeply offended, not by being called Dr. Angst but by being noticed that much. Words began to spill out of me, quite out of my control. "Why try to know anything about a place? The customs, the size, the weather, the people, the economy, the politics, the fish, the suntan techniques, the games, the swimming. It is better to stay indoors and not mess around with useless experiences. A small room in a boarding house. Anonymous. Eat each meal at a plastic counter. Smitty's will do. Do nothing, want nothing, if you feel like walking, walk; sleeping, sleep. Do you know how hard that is? No memories; if they start to intrude, invent them. Three is sufficient. I use only three. New York for adventure, beaches for relaxation, the octopus and Nog for speculation. No connections. Narrow all possibilities. Develop and love your limitations. No one knows you. Know no one. Natural rhythms, my dear. That's the ticket."

She had wandered off to pick up a mussel shell. She came skipping back. "I use them for collages. I paste them in; shells, colored pieces of glass, driftwood, anything." She giggled. "Did you know that today is the Fourth of July?"

"No."

"We're having a party. You're invited. Everyone is coming. Well, not *everyone,* but Timmons and Harry and the man who runs the gift shop and one or two others. My husband too, of course."

I put my arm around her. Her behavior seemed to allow for such an embrace as long as nothing called her attention to it. But she stepped away, giving me a quizzical glance. I am unable to cope with quizzical glances.

"I know you," I said decisively, trying to struggle away. "Ten years ago in New York; I don't remember your name, but I *might* have even slept with you. It scares me, stumbling onto a part of my past like that.

You were more emaciated then, of course, with your hair very ratty. You were carrying a sign in some kind of demonstration when I met you, that's you, very political. Am I right?"

"I'm from Baltimore," she said with a quick glance down at her awful feet. "I've never seen a demonstration of any kind. We moved out here when Ollie got a job working with an agricultural firm. They transferred him. We like it fine."

"I won't press," I said. I have retained a certain amount of old-fashioned dignity. "Who you are and what you do are your problems."

We walked on in silence. The silence, in fact, was fierce. And, I was proud to think, not one piece of information had I given away. No history, therefore no bondage. I have known myself to give out with facts, numbers, names, stories. I am that nervous sometimes. But as I said before, I am faster now. It was a joy to walk beside her with only her self-conscious distrust of me to handle. She was thinking I was only a little weird, possibly diseased; she was too simple, too nice to think anything more. And I'm too haggard to produce sexual fears; my ears are too huge and my lips too thin and uncontrolled.

We pressed on in the rain. I was all for delaying the walk as much as possible, but she was too determined to get home. Just before the house she had proudly marked as hers, we passed an old man in a First World War hat, struggling with a heavy log. He was bent and puffing as he tried to shift the log on top of a low makeshift sea wall.

I stopped. He was remarkably ugly and defiant.

"Colonel Green," the girl said. "He lives in that big three-story house next to ours. He has a grandson in there and some kind of a woman, but they hardly ever show themselves. It's not a good policy to talk to him. He comes out in every storm. A maniac about the sea. He must be eighty, honest, and Ollie says that all that's keeping him alive is this crazy war he has going against the sea. Everyone thinks he's a blight on the community."

"Grab hold," Colonel Green ordered. He marched up and shouted in my ear. "Goddamn water rising at three hundred miles an hour. Too dumb to see it? Flood the whole town before anyone shifts ass to do anything about it. Fact. Lift her up."

I helped him lift the log onto the sea wall. He was dressed in a yellow mackintosh and big fishing boots. His furiously weathered face was sunk deep into his neck, and his tiny blue eyes, like two pale robin's eggs, protruded into the night, unblinking and beautiful.

"People," he yelled again into my ear.

I helped him with another log. We labored and swore, but the log kept slipping back onto the sand. Finally the colonel ordered a halt and sat down on the sea wall, wheezing and kicking the wet sand with his boots. I could only pick out every third or fourth word the colonel said, the wind was so strong and his voice had sunk to such a rasp. "Hear . . . no retreat . . . only . . . bastard sea . . . kicking up higher . . . iron woman . . . What . . . ? What . . .? What . . . ?"

I went up and yelled in his ear. "Right. A huge operation. Biggest operation in years. Massive. Mounting up out there. Ready to initiate general collapse. *Any*time."

We yelled back and forth. Then he punched me amiably in the stomach, and we struggled with the log. This time we made it. After another rest, we walked down to the sea for a better evaluation. "Jeep," the colonel yelled, coming up to my ear again and grasping me by the neck so I wouldn't turn away. He only had, after all, so many words in him. "Good thick sand tires. Drag every piece of maverick wood to the stronghold. Dig in! Protect the road!"

I nodded and followed him up the beach to his house. Before very long, however, I took a sharp turn to the left and ducked out of his line of march. As it happened, I was unfortunate enough to be standing in front of the girl's large bay window. She was standing with several other people, looking gaily down at me. I didn't, of course, want to have anything to do with anyone. The evening had already been too much of a lark. It might possibly set me back for months. I wanted only to get to bed and pull the covers over my head. A few sips of whiskey, that would do me fine. Just to listen to the storm with a memory or two. To go over once again a few details about the octopus. My clothes were drenched. I had long ago taken off my shoes and shirt. I was suffering from chills. They were waving. But I wasn't going anywhere. I had done very well that night. I had talked far too much but was rather amazed at how well I had managed. Nothing had been said. It was all right.

A hand grabbed the upper part of my arm and escorted me into the house.

"It's about time," a low, modulated, terrifically friendly voice roared. "I'm Ollie, of course. *Glad* to have you aboard. You're quite the stranger around here. I won't even ask what you were doing with that old maniac out there. It looks like we got to you just in time. What's that? Look here, Sarah, this poor fella has had it. Get him some dry clothes. Better still, get him into my terrycloth bathrobe. That's it. Get in there now. That's the boy."

I followed Sarah into the bedroom. She smiled at me, and I took off my clothes.

"Now wait," she said, very fast. "Listen. I don't know you. That bathrobe. The bathrobe is hanging in the bathroom."

I went into the bathroom and stood, shivering, behind the door. I too was a little ill at ease. After all, at first sight I've been told I'm not exactly pleasing to look at. "I was a track man," I yelled into the bedroom. "Four-forty under fifty-five seconds. I assure you." There was no answer. There didn't seem to be anything else to do but to give out with some information. "Slipping out from New York, everything going too fast. Left and wandered out to Coast. Met Nog and bought octopus. Traveled to county and state fairs, developing wonderful aversion to people and trips in general but at the same time a growing obsession with octopus. Hard to even talk about it. Was afraid to let go, surrender it, walk away. Settled down here just to sit, you understand, wanting nothing at all. Waiting it out. Then thinking of beaches, developing that memory up to par with other two. Beaches, you understand, beaches where most of life has dribbled away, past beaches, future beaches and now right here a . . ."

I ventured a peek out the door, but she had left the bedroom. I preferred to think she hadn't heard me; that, indeed, she had never heard me. I could still slip out. The terrycloth bathrobe was hanging behind the door. I put it on and turned to investigate the bathroom. It was a beautiful bathroom. There was a huge green tile tub, a new toilet and washbowl. I opened the cabinet over the washbowl. I couldn't stop looking at the objects on the top two shelves: suntan oil, Anacins, cold cream, three pink hair curlers, two yellow toothbrushes, one of which was very dirty, Dramamine pills, Itolsol eye bath, Ban, Kolex cold capsules, Ammens Medicated Powder and a small box of Benzedrine pills. I stared at each object and then went over them again. A bottle of hydrogen peroxide fell from one of the lower shelves. I dumped the contents of every bottle in the cabinet into the bathtub except for the Benzedrine pills, which I put into the pocket of the terrycloth bathrobe. I turned the water on. It was a reviving thing to do. Then I turned the water off and stepped into the bedroom. The bedroom was painted a pale mauve. There was a king-sized bed, three small watercolors of clipper ships, a dresser, a sewing machine, two night tables and a television set. It was pleasant. I felt very relaxed. I got into bed and pulled the covers over my head.

I thought of Nog. He would be wandering over the Sierras probably, that yellow light streaming from his chest. I haven't been able to think too clearly about the octopus since I had come to the beach. I had given it a chance, it wasn't as if I had deserted it. I had driven through the Northwest, the Southwest and the Midwest. Thousands of people had looked at it, and many had even thought it was real. I had made money. But once off the road I could never go out behind the boarding house and look at it up on the truck bed. It was the last thing to throw away. Lately I've imagined its eight tentacles wrapped around my head, slowly smothering me.

I must have fallen asleep. A hand shook me. "Now look. It's perfectly all right if you come in and use my terrycloth bathrobe and even take a nap in the middle of my bed, but why violate my bathroom?"

I slipped my head under the covers.

Ollie pulled the covers off the bed. I looked up at his face.

It wasn't too bad a face. It was broad and handsome in a puffy way. Ollie was about to say something when Sarah took him by the hand and led him to the doorway. They whispered together. Finally Sarah came back and said, sweetly, "I'll bet you would like to join the party. We're going to have fireworks. Please, it will be fun."

Between the two of them I was escorted to the edge of the living-room rug. There were five people. There might have been more in other rooms, but I counted five. I took care not to notice anything else. I sat down.

"The last time was in New York," I said.

"Is that right," a fat man said. He was eating an egg- and shrimp-salad sandwich and drinking bourbon and water.

"New York is an active place. Not as much action as you might have been led to believe, but still, an active place. I lived in a sort of penthouse. Beautiful furniture. Turn-of-the-century stuff."

"What exactly is your line?" I was asked.

"I'm a cultural impresario. Nog is the name. I'm investigating cephalopods or, as they say here, octopi or octopuses. Timid creatures, really, much maligned."

The man excused himself and went into the next room.

The wind battered against the window. I remember that very well, the wind battering against the window and the hum of conversation. I pulled the curtain over the bay window to protect the room from the terrible racket of the storm.

There was boisterous talk about fireworks and drinking and last year's Fourth of July party.

Sarah advanced towards me, smiling bravely, "Having fun?" she asked.

"Of course I'm having fun," I replied.

"Would you mind telling me what you do?" she asked.

It was obvious that they were closing in on me. I was forced to throw out a series of delaying actions.

"You may ask," I said, being extremely polite. "Of course you may ask. I'm making a survey of the West Coast. Marine animals mostly. Did you know fossils of cephalopods have been found in rocks that are believed to be at least four hundred million years old? They are harmless. Most people don't want to know that, but they are harmless, even rather stupid . . . I am also making a survey of the Sierras and another, more general survey, on Los Angeles, Sacramento, Portland, Seattle, San Francisco, Oakland and Santa Barbara, to name a few. I am also, on the side, so to speak, investigating totems."

I remember dancing.

I remember sitting for a long stretch, looking at television.

I was able to become more anonymous. I ate roast beef and drank Seven-Up.

I remember no more until I was asked down to the game room by Ollie. "Now, Mr. Mysterious," he said, laughing and slapping me on the back. "You can tell me what you do."

"A survey of beaches," I replied quickly. "Taking ten to fifteen years. The best years of my life consumed in this project. All over the Western world. Marvelous and fantastic stories. Over eight beaches noted so far, actually eighty-seven. To name a few: Far Rockaway, Montauk, Las Palmas, Harrison's Landing, Brighton, Antibes, Westhampton, Orient, Marblehead, Malibu, Coventry, Truro, the whole area of the Ceylonese coast, Tangier, Tunis and Ceuta, that whole stretch, Ibiza and Formentera, Vancouver and two beaches in Rhodes and Hydra, three in Crete and only one in all of Ireland. The beach here, the present one, is calm, wide and sandy, few sharks, and a good class of swimmers. Weather mostly good. Except, of course, for tonight. Tonight there is a storm."

He handed me a Ping-Pong racket. We played Ping-Pong.

At first I just shoveled the ball back, trying to be polite. I managed to get the ball close to his racket.

But then he grew angry and shouted at me to play ball. I put little twists on the ball and chopped back on the serve. He slammed back harder. Several times it appeared that he wanted to say something, but we were playing so hard there was no time to talk. I kept him hopping. There were backhand smashes for him to contend with, forehand chops, tricky cross-court serves, sleezy slices. Balls sprayed around the room, but he had a plentiful supply from a large wicker basket that hung from the ceiling on a wire chain. We played even harder, and I rolled up the sleeves of my terrycloth bathrobe. Finally, wheezing and perspiring, he stood still, squeezing a Ping-Pong ball in his hand. He appeared to be stuck in some way. There was nothing else to do but grab the basket of Ping-Pong balls and fling them at him. That started him off. He yelled. I threw my paddle, catching him in the throat. Then I tipped over the table. He was left sitting on the floor.

I walked out of the game room and into the storm.

Colonel Green was still working on the sea wall. He had managed to move one more log.

"Getting you down?" I yelled at him. "Worst storm in years. Watch battle fatigue. Absolutely all right."

The colonel surveyed the beach, his hands on his hips.

"Crashing . . . now . . . 1937 . . . the drift . . . up later . . . no help . . . tatters . . . tatters . . ."

I grabbed the end of a log. "Where do you get these logs?" I yelled. "What do you do, push them back when the storm is over?"

"Selfish . . . 1937 . . . four-door sedan . . . stand tall . . ."

We labored some more but couldn't move the log. I went back to my room and went to bed.

What I should have done was get rid of the octopus, what I have been trying to do is get rid of the octopus, what I am beginning just now to remember was that I did get rid of the octopus. I see it now for the first time. I either took it back to the party and put it in the bathtub or danced with it on the beach. No, I did bring it back to the beach but not to dance with. I took off my terrycloth bathrobe and ran down to the truck and got the octopus out of the bathysphere, its tentacles waving all over me. Struggling in the rain and wind, I dragged it back and pulled it up on the sea wall. Such a spectator gave the colonel enough of a jolt to finish the sea wall. Then together we threw it in the sea, and I went home and went to bed. It was something like that, I can remember something like that, a storm, a party and then the octopus. There was an octopus, although I know deep down that the octopus is still up on blocks. I know, too, that nothing happened and I haven't traveled with the octopus. But I shall move on anyway, perhaps to New York. I remember great things about New York.

I ran down to the sea. I took off a shoe and shoved a foot in. There was a quickness, certainly, a sudden delirium, as if I were about to be sure of something. But it's out of my depth to run down to the sea and make a report. The only clarity is in the morning air. But as my foot grew colder, a warmth appeared, a flush to the cheeks, and there is something to say, right now, but my voice doesn't have the momentum. I am too comfortable sitting on the sand, my foot drying now, not knowing that I am about to move on. The storm wasn't invented. I'm sure of that. And the sea was cold and even wet. That was two or three days ago. But there must be another place, a replacement, one foot having the problem of following the other foot, to another place. Now that there are no other feet to follow. I stood and sat again. I must be holding back. I'm breathing easier, trying to watch or not to watch, my suitcase next to me and my frozen foot withdrawing from the sea and entering the sock and then the shoe. There is no sound within, although I'm lighter. I haven't eaten in days. The day is lighter than the day before. I might manage a bark. But I have to watch that. I don't have to bark against the sound of waves. I must be moving on. I turned my back to the sea. I stood facing the road. Orange and black butterflies glided through the eucalyptus trees. I was holding back, but I knew I had moved on long before, years before, despite my calm breathing in and out, my suitcase ready to be grasped—and I did grasp it, and my foot, as if by itself, took a step and I was moving on, up the beach, past the sea wall, to the edge of the road.

I hitchhiked to San Francisco.

I was let off near a supermarket. It was dark. I was standing comfortably enough, looking at the neon lights, but I needed a direction, the hint of some discernible habit, a movement of some kind. A place to stand but at the same time to appear busy. I have no memories, only vague symbols of separations: an overturned kitchen table, a ripped bed sheet, a broken battleship abandoned at the bottom of a bathtub. I went into the supermarket. The aisles were crowded with evening shoppers. There was Muzak. I slid into the warm colors and the clicks of the cash registers. I tried to remember near the frozen foods, I am trying to remember, what it was I had to remember, but I had forgotten what I had gone in for, what it is exactly I have to go out for. I pushed the cart down the length of one aisle and halfway up another. I picked up a can of beans. I must have picked up a can of beans because I can remember putting a can of beans back on the shelf and picking up another, a bottle of beans. I put the bottle of beans near cans of chop suey and vegetables and Pet milk. Then, finally, I managed to hold two cans of tuna fish. Something was evoked. A meal. Mayonnaise and onions and tuna fish in London, New York or Palma. It doesn't matter. I put the two cans of tuna fish in the cart and pushed on, past plastic toys, light bulbs and electrical fixtures. A red can opener held me for several minutes. I put it in the cart and pushed on. I paused near the meat counter, my eyes locked by a delicate set of fingers stuffing a package of lamb chops into the large pocket of a yellow rain slicker. The slicker was unbuttoned. Inside was a faded blue-flowered print dress. Her thick blond hair flowed loosely to her waist. He shorts legs were awkward around the kneecaps, as if somehow splayed, but her wide stance was vulnerable enough to be exciting. Red plastic shoes with stubby tips covered her feet. I watched her fingers calmly drop pork chops into a straw basket followed by several pounds of spareribs. I delayed looking at her face. I concentrated on the foods in my cart and pushed forward until the cart came to rest against her thighs. She turned. There is no focus to her face; her features are broad and healthy, no doubt lovely, call them lovely, but I don't know where to start, how to approach the small stubborn nose, the unparted lips, the eyes are fading, looking at me but fading, and my own eyes have become glazed. I started at a point between her eyes. She didn't smile or show any surprise, perhaps because there was no motion at all to my own face, or so I thought. I have been wrong about that before. She moved to the side slowly and deliberately, as if completing a step in a formal dance. She stood in front of the cold cuts. I too made a move, as if responding to the same conductor, to a position in front of the fish, to her right. I picked up a flounder, holding it for a moment so that it draped over my hand. Then I slipped the flounder under my shirt. It was remarkably cold, but I remained silent. She moved on and I have moved on, not knowing if I am following or if she is following or perhaps if in some way we are moving parallel to each other. I stopped for a bottle of artichoke hearts, slipping them into my jacket pocket. When I looked up, she had disappeared. The separation is not acute. At least I managed to inhabit, for a brief moment, a friendly and detached space in front of the meat counter. I was quiet, but I have thought and been suspicious about silence a long time. There are certain moments, after an estrangement, when my cock shrivels up into my body. No, that's not it. It has nothing to do with that. I'm grazing. I should have pinioned her with the cart and slipped it into her as she was bending over the meat counter. Never mind the rest. She might not have noticed. She hasn't noticed. The neutrality must have been the seduction. I pushed on, filling my cart with orange juice, milk, eggs and cheese. Foods with no smell, cool to the touch. Her eyes had been very blue, as if far-reaching, like the eyes of Nog. (Eyes I have known.) But her eyes were dim, faded. The memories will come, are coming, lists of separations, arrivals. I don't have to rush it. Nog has not disappeared. Only memory survives. Her obtuse eyes reflected a quest, if only for meat, but even so, a quest. And Nog is on a quest of obsessive walking and sleeping between dog-eaten blankets on splintered floors. I can't see farther than that. She had turned away, there is no mistaking that, but something happened or at least was noted. Not an understanding, I'm not frantic enough to suspect that, but perhaps a paranoia, a shared paralysis, a delicate and withdrawn . . . It doesn't matter. I found her again on another aisle. I noticed a head of lettuce in her cart and two avocados. I picked up a bottle of crab-meat cocktail, two cans of smoked oysters and a can of chicken salad that I had no particular interest in. I remember filling both pockets of my pants with tartar sauce, onion flakes and paprika. I was not altogether unaware that this might be a setup, that I might be fingered for some kind of a mark or a bust. I dumped everything in the nearest cart except two pads of butter, a container of milk and a small bottle of artichoke hearts. I kept the flounder inside my shirt. Dampness keeps me in tune, focused on the task at hand, on the possibility of a progression, on the hope that there is, in fact, a task. We moved towards the checkout counter. I was open, ready for her to reveal herself, to move forward or backward, to hunt or flee. I am still open, lying as if in wait for something or someone. But it was confusing, people became blurred, the aisles without end, almost circular, the food suddenly animate, fields of waving coffee cans, rows of sweating lemons and expanding lettuce, shifting piles of bananas and candy bars and the food in my own cart huddling together, as if for warmth, minuscule and afraid. I was at the checkout counter, moving through, pushing away a delirium tremens, and nothing was happening. I paid, gratefully, and she paid too, just in front of me, for the lettuce and two avocados, her pockets bulging, her straw basket full and the huge mirror overhead reflecting all. But then we were on the street. Everything eventually finds its way to the street. We walked. She stopped in the middle of an empty parking lot and let her limp hand drop into mine. Kissing the lobe of an ear, she confessed that just to keep in shape, so to speak, to keep herself in control, she turned occasional tricks with the managers of two supermarkets.

From my window, which extends to the floor, I can see a bridge and several round hills. The bridge looks familiar. I suspect that I'm in San Francisco. It was dark when Meridith led me away from the supermarket two or three days ago. I have been lying on my mattress, jerking off. The bridge in New York bound and twisted two shores together, making the ugly rush of water insistent and brutal. Bodies floated against the pilings. I've flirted with that memory before. It doesn't work as a catalyst. But I can remember how Meridith handed me the straw basket and I emptied my food into it, including the flounder. She wanted to touch each object, to feel its weight and size. She walked on. I followed, carrying the basket. I have left Barcelona and Kuwait without knowing I was leaving. I need a list of departures to keep suspended my own sense of arrival. But they fail, my head fails, my steps succeeded and we came to a three-story house in a commercial neighborhood: empty and abandoned stores, warehouses, a gas station on one corner, a Mexican bar on the other. A street light shone a block away. The house is wooden and old. The front step is caved in. I remembered, stepping over the step, that I had left my suitcase on the side of the road. Either that or in front of the supermarket. I sat down on the last step as Meridith went inside. I took out each object in the basket and slowly put them back, one by one. I had a ride in a blue pickup truck. I kept my eyes on the mile gauge, touching the side of the door as each mile came and went. The night of the storm is returning. I haven't asked for that. I can remember the television set and the octopus and the heavy weight of its tentacles. The tentacles were too long. They drooped. They got in the way. Losing my clothes and shaving kit doesn't bother me. But the suitcase itself, with the stickers and dents on it, was a record, a map I could retrace and run my fingers over whenever I wanted to. Sitting on the front step, I was afraid to go inside, to enter a space alone without a change of underwear or stickers, a lid to snap open or close, a weight to complain about. But I had the straw basket. That was enough of a ticket. I looked through my wallet. There were three carefully folded chewing-gum wrappers, the Oregon driver's license made out to Orin Carmele, an address of a hitchhiker from Cody, Wyoming, two white pills, half a snapshot of a small sailboat, an empty air-mail stamp book, a flat fold of tin foil and three ripped movie stubs. I put everything but the forty-eight dollars into the straw basket. Entrances are always hard, never moist or dewy enough. Once inside, there is hopefully enough natural movement, enough frenzied propulsion to find a way out. I have entered a swimming pool in Palm Springs, a small hand on my wrist, and gone straight to the bottom. I have entered without hesitation Radio City Music Hall in the morning and either Susan or Ann. I have not left anything behind except for the suitcase and possibly the octopus and truck. That might reveal itself to me by degrees. There is plenty of time for that. I don't want to rush anything. I want to forget more than I remember. Last night and the immediate nights before can be suspended, until I go limp enough not to notice myself, to lose control. I touched the side of the house. Flakes of yellow paint fell off in my fingers. I could enter the house because with the basket I would be unnoticed, like a delivery boy, and would fall out as fast as I fell in. I did go inside, carrying the basket in front of me with both hands. I tried to keep from whistling, but a sound emerged, a soft two-note in a minor key. The long hall smelled of cat sperm and was lighted by candles placed in holes chiseled in the wall. There were posters of rock-'n'-roll groups and children's drawings on yellow lined paper. There appeared to be poems scotch-taped here and there, but I didn't want to look too closely. I walked straight to the end of the hall without stopping. I entered the kitchen. I lowered the basket next to the icebox and sat down at a large wooden table with initials and words carved deeply into it. The words were mostly one-syllabled: sky, wood, card, cunt, river, hat, bag, mountain, beach, fuck, town, sand, gun, soldier, sailor, Indian chief, car, boat, plane, walk, fire, plants, snake, skull, brother, sister, father, mother. I read every initial and word, at the same time noticing hands reach methodically into a huge wooden salad bowl and withdraw pieces of lettuce, tomatoes, avocados, artichoke hearts, boiled eggs, onions, scallions, carrots and anchovies. Five men and three women were seated at the table. Three of the men had shoulder-length hair, and four of them had thick mustaches turning downwards at the edge of their mouths. I made the count several times. Two wore small blue pinch-brim caps with glass beads on the top. The women wore simple print dresses and no make-up, and the men blue jeans and faded work shirts. Everyone wore medallions around their necks. One woman nursed a baby, while the other two slowly shelled peas into a metal bowl. The men sat silently, their eyes blank, reaching out to eat from the bowl. They seem young although it is hard to tell. I seem young although it is hard to tell. I ate a tomato and a carrot and, very quickly, a handful of lettuce and boiled egg. I was hungry. No one seemed to notice me, or if they did they offered no sign. I ate steadily. I felt once a need to say something, to make some gesture, however small. But I could only eat. There were moments when I forgot anyone else was around. The bowl empty, I managed a low hum, a sound that has often signified a need for attention or a diversion from attention. A man stood up, slowly stretched, said "Later" and left. Another carved a word or initial into the table with a bowie knife. The women discussed the large amount of laundry and the diminishing food supply in the pantry. Meridith came in. She put her hands on my shoulders and slowly massaged the back of my neck. My head sagged. I struggled against giving in, against dropping to the floor. Her arms circled my neck, her hands groping my face as if she were blind. Through her sweaty fingers I saw a man begin to draw circles on a piece of white paper with green and yellow crayons. Her arms remind me of tentacles. Her breath on my neck is warm—a faint beginning, a dry sirocco, a labored breathing, a caress. I must not remember places. I have no need for beaches, parks, luncheonettes, cities, rooms, corners, attics, streets or rivers now that I am in a place. I have pulled down the shade. I don't need a bridge, only her breath in and out against my rigid neck and the tide going in and out as once, at anchor, I indulged the tea treatment, off the coast of . . . no, that's no longer necessary. I read the manual. First tea, then a dash of cold water, then hot tea. Then cold water, squirting it in with my mouth, slowly. Slowly. Endless alterations. She loved it, moaning over and over: there's a mad joy to the son of a bitch. I was entertaining myself, I hadn't forgotten, spreading her legs on the bunk, the liquid streaming down her thighs, kneeling before her, the captain pacing on the deck overhead, squirting it into her, even rhythms, that's the ticket, shooting it in and one and two and hold it, darling, hear the tide changing, and three and four, we're coming around and one and two and I did have an effect, suddenly, that long ago. I don't remember any more. Meridith's hands rested on my shoulders.

Perhaps, even now, she is thinking of me. There have been other services, given and rendered, three-day passes, other inventions and manuals and I must find something, now that the others are slipping, have perhaps slipped away.

I have said it all before: having come to this house, some time ago, but first having crossed the country, wandering around, for a year, two years or perhaps longer. Perhaps, having said it before, this is the end. Perhaps pulling down the shade is the end. How am I to know except by looking back if I am settled or not? I am not thinking about going on or not going on. There is no anguish, no confusion even though I don't remember what happened last night after leaving the kitchen. Is that where the anguish lies, caked near the stopper? I do remember. I took a bath. Somewhere in the distance between the twisted blue sock in the corner and the window sill I can remember. I am going too fast and not fast enough, past the sound of speed or past the movement of the earth and yet I'm not moving at all.

"Time to get pumpkins," a man said. "In the moonlight you can pick em out. They squat there by the hundreds. Should get us forty to fifty."

Everyone left except the girl nursing the baby and Meridith. Meridith went to the icebox and came back with a small jar of artichoke hearts. She sat down beside me. She made no sound when she chewed. For that I am grateful.

The girl nursing the baby sighed. She was very thin, almost skeletal, with long stringy black hair and large brown eyes. Underneath her yellow dress she wore black stockings. Her mouth was thin and set in an expression of subdued pain. Two men came in. They sat down. Then one of them left.

"I can't handle certain things," the girl said, looking at Meridith. "I should take something or just keep quiet for a few days. Maybe it's nursing. I don't know. I might have to leave. A flower came at me yesterday when I was lying in bed. It came down from the ceiling. A few feet from my face it turned into a black umbrella. The umbrella just stayed there, it wasn't even raining, but then it became a mushroom and the mushroom got closer and closer. I had to get up and walk around. I didn't know where I was . . . This afternoon I was bouncing on the trampoline. My body needs it and it's therapeutic. I was going higher and higher and suddenly there was this enormous black bird, like a pelican, right over me, opening its mouth. The mouth kept getting bigger and bigger. It was very real. But I kept jumping up and down even though I wanted to run inside. Henry joined me and started jumping alongside me and I told him about the bird. He held my hand and the bird flew up a few feet. But it was still there. Then he put his finger inside me at the top of a jump and he kept it in as we went down and then up again and on top of the jump the bird wasn't there. We lay on the trampoline and he made it with me. Then he did a backward somersault over the side of the trampoline and I haven't seen him since. But I'm afraid of closing my eyes. I see things when I close my eyes."

She removed the baby from her nipple and placed him on his stomach on the table. Then she changed his diaper. She didn't look at anyone. When she had finished with the diaper she picked the baby up and left. The man had gone to the stove and was making a stew.

Meridith, paused, holding an artichoke between thumb and forefinger. "Would you like a bath?" she asked. "You must be tired. Or would you rather split? Someone is probably expecting you somewhere."

"I would just as soon stay on," I said.

She walked over to a loudspeaker on the side of the wall near the icebox. She pushed a button and said into a small phone next to the speaker, "One for the top floor." She pushed another button, and the reply came: "Room twenty-six. Name?"

Meridith looked at me.

"Nog," I said.

She repeated the name and then came over to me and took me by the hand. We went down the hall. She stopped. "What kind of music would you like?" she asked.

"Chants are okay," I said. "Anything with not too many words."

We went back to the kitchen. She said into the phone, "Chants for the bath." We returned down the hall. I followed her down dark winding steps to a large cavernous room dimly lit by a kerosene lamp. There were three concrete tubs, about ten feet long and five feet wide, and two smaller, regular-sized tubs. The floor was concrete and covered with an inch of water. We took our clothes off and laid them on a wooden bench. It was very warm. A low Gregorian chant filled the room. Two heads were visible in one of the tubs, and a large foot resting on the edge. A man lay on his stomach on a wooden table. The air smelled of ammonia. Meridith turned a switch near the door. A soft liquid light on the ceiling flashed slowly around.

We stood, looking each other over, I suppose, although the light, like the revolving beam on top of police cars, made her seem mysterious and unapproachable. Her breasts were small and firm and her hips large.

We climbed into the tub nearest the far wall.

If I had fewer limbs, if I had been in some way maimed on the road or a victim of an accident, I would be more prepared. As it is, I have to invent my way into situations. It never hurts to have a story prepared, a memory, any kind of wrong information; to be ready to go forward or backward at the least suspicious move. The more sympathy enlisted, the more easily one can receive service and relaxation. But I have a suntan and a spring to my step. No, I'm pale and emaciated, but my body felt tan, even resonant, as I climbed into the tub. There are times when the voice of the narrator or the presence of the narrator should almost sing out.

Meridith's neck and head were above the water. The water seemed to be perfumed. I sat opposite her, my back against the edge. My skin felt soft, like mother-of-pearl. I reached out a foot and touched her thigh. Memories can be vast and delicious. The touch of one, like a favorite stone or shell, can balance the worst of looks. I wasn't having any trouble creating a protective covering. I wanted to say something formal, to balance my hysterical foot rubbing against her ass. "On the last beach I was face to face with a minor discovery, but now I'm beginning to inhabit that discovery. It's not that nature went mad before man did, but it's that life's principle is to make shells."

Meridith slid an arm around my stomach. A leg touched mine. She seemed to be half kneeling before me, her head bent so that her thick wet hair looked for a moment like a dome. I felt as if I were being slowly encircled. I held on to one of her nipples. "Shells are bits of man and bits of woman," I said. "The beach is a boneyard."

She bit me on the neck.

I remembered the storm, or I can remember it now, how the wind suddenly changed and the octopus flapped on top of the sea wall. I lost something, and this is the beginning of something else. It will take its own time. Her arms and legs embraced me, her mouth sucked at mine and I remembered lying on the beach, the wind whipping at me, my clothes heavy with water. I threw the octopus into a wave, but it was picked up and swept back, curled over on the beach, its tentacles torn off, the round hump battered and disfigured. I heard a soft splash. Someone else was in the tub. The light continued to revolve and I watched it, my cock now expanded despite the hot water, but not knowing for sure if I was inside Meridith. Her tongue was active. There was another splash. A large foot placed itself in the center of my back. "Give me some of that," I heard a voice say. I was pinned by several sets of legs. The chanting had stopped, but someone was talking very specifically about a naval battle off the coast of Brazil. I sank deeper. Hands rubbed me, soaping my hair, my stomach, my balls, my feet. I felt as if I were burrowing into a center, or perhaps I was being mutilated in some way in preparation to being swallowed. But tentacles were all around me and I was being munched on. And suddenly I came alive, or I came and I was dead and I only heard a faint humming as if reaching me down miles and miles of spirals.

I managed to extract myself. I was finished anyway. No one seemed to notice me climb out. I picked up the first set of clothes I came to. A pair of blue jeans, a khaki shirt and black boots. They were all too big, but I climbed the stairs without any trouble.

I would like to stay, certainly, not to move on, to allow nothing to happen while waiting for something to happen, to lie in front of the window now that I have the shade pulled. And so far I haven't said who I was, where I was going. I haven't given out with any information. Or rather, I have. I goofed. It was Nog. Nog survived. I'm stuck with Nog. Days have gone by. I haven't been out of the room. There is a loudspeaker on the wall and music and sometimes voices. In the early morning, exercises come across: ho ho hram hrim hrum hrah. The room is empty except for my mattress and the night table where the tray of food is left. The walls are white and the window sills pale blue. If I had fewer limbs, but I said that. There are certain repetitions that don't work. I used to turn a corner and expect wherever I was staying to have disappeared, and I would split to defeat the expectation. I must dare not to be fathomed. I must not let myself be known, in order to know myself. There are variations. I like the sound of them all. I am not involved in the process of change, but it is important that I see someone, to share this change. It is not crucial to know with whom. But it's probably necessary to spend time with whoever it is, before moving on. Perhaps with Meridith or the man who brings the tray. The octopus has disintegrated. But I haven't thought of that since the bath. I am very clean.

The loudspeaker reports a meeting in the living room. It is the seventh meeting in the living room in the last few days. There have also been meetings, gatherings and mergings in the kitchen, dining room, pantry and hallway on the second floor.

Nog was as comfortable inside as he was outside. I might as well get on with him. He could stand as well as sit before nothing in particular. Despite what he said, he could entertain himself. It's necessary now not to believe the memory of him, in order to develop it further. There is no need to name streets or waterfalls. He doesn't notice them that way. Recently he has become easily lost. I have an urge to listen to the sound of his breathing, of my breathing and balance myself between the two, between the sock and the mattress and to notice the distance that has been covered. That is not alarming because I plan to move on, to erase the distances just covered, perhaps to the kitchen, perhaps down the hall. In any case, soon.

LOOKING back, Nog appears, leaning against a cottonwood or redwood or piñon tree . . . by a small stream in the foothills. He is dusty and half dead, his horse, a pinto or appaloosa, drinks beside him. He wears chaps and a torn shirt made out of deer hide, his six-shooter notched, ready to . . . no, that's too far back. He turns on under the calligraphy of vapor trails fifteen thousand feet high. He knows the mountains were formed from glaciers because he has traced the passage of the ice with his fingers. Oranges and Tillamook cheese are on the table, a fire in the wood stove, a woman's heavy thighs visible as she bends to feed the chickens. He is tired. He has stolen a stick of dynamite from a logging company and blown off the side of a small hill. A wild goat was standing on the small hill, at the time. In the city he wears a clear red flannel shirt, brown corduroy pants, scuffed black boots. He stands on the corner not waiting or listening.

To do it, to wait in the middle of the mattress, as places drop away, to wait for Nog. It's too big a breath. I am bound not to hold it, to forget. I did forget. Lockett interrupted me. Lockett is Meridith's husband. Or at least he knows her. He has made films of her or he owns films of her. He dresses in faded white jeans and immaculate white tee shirt. He has no mustache or snap-brim cap. He has narrow features, an affable, unassuming manner . . . no, that's terrible . . . He is emaciated. His curly black hair falls to his shoulders, framing a ravaged face, a face eaten into by long passages of uncontrollable enthusiasm or despair. What few teeth he has left in his loose flapping mouth are blunted and yellow.

"Known a heap of women," Lockett says. He sits in the corner and stares at his bare feet. His boots stand upright by the door. "Women out of Santa Fe, Carson City, Needles. You name it. I've got film footage of Meridith. Used to be she called me the Torpor Kid, account of I'd hunker down to a cup of black coffee to no effect, just to nod out. Riled her to see me nod out. I was in from homesteading in northern Idaho first I took up with her. Nothing for hundreds of miles in northern Idaho. Space like that drives a man crazy or to sheep. Course I couldn't take not knowing why I was there in the first place. No reason to take it. No reason to take much of anything."

I try to tell Lockett, try to get through to him about logging in Oregon, about building the octopus and traveling around with it and finally selling it. Then blowing up the side of a hill just to blow up the side of a hill. But he interrupts, talking about Meridith as though no one, not even himself, can overhear.

"Don't fall out on me. Listen. I was standing. Might have been waiting. Don't recollect. She leaned against me, you understand . . . I was outside this supermarket, having hitchhiked in from northern Idaho. Maybe, just to think on it, I had been around for a while. But it was that late time of day when you're waiting for something to happen and it hasn't happened and you don't care any more. Last job I had was like that, fixing chimneys from Seattle on down the Coast. I'd climb up to demonstrate how the chimney needed repair, and in the process knock off a few bricks. I'd be up there on the roof and forget why I was knocking down this chimney . . . I'll never work again. I'm going to be demonstrating my own self now . . . So she comes out of the supermarket and leans on me. Just like that. She had a big basket of food and she gives me that look that has no inside to it, no reach, and I touched her. Figured she was somebody passing through. Never known me to turn down a trick like that. I followed her into a parking lot. She smiled and we got into this yellow convertible. Fifty miles later, her hand working me over, I learn it's not her car. We take a right turn and head up into the Sierras, where this family I know lives. Nothing more than a couple of shacks. We stay on. Must have been six or seven of us. Others came and went. Meridith doesn't say a word for forty-seven days, and I like to choke her to death. She put me through some changes. Right when I get to thinking I might be used to her, that there was no reason she should be saying anything, we lit out and come down here. Someone said the place was about to get busted. It was time to leave anyway . . ."

Lockett first came into my room two days ago; no, it was yesterday. He has come in and out so often . . . It is evening. It is difficult to know the time with the shade down and now a thick blanket over the shade. He enters without knocking. I appreciate that. He has no sense of transitions. He walks slowly around the mattress, staring down like a pool player approaching a hard combination. Then he shows the film. He has shown it a dozen times. It is grainy and out of focus. He shows it against the wall, in eight millimeter. While it's running, he either folds his arms around his chest and rocks back and forth, staring at it, or he chisels a hole in the wall for a small candle. There are now seven holes in the wall.

Meridith stands in front of the camera and slowly takes off her clothes, letting them drop at her feet. She looks younger, her breasts firmer, her gaze deliberate and self-conscious. She pouts as she waters potted ferns on the window sill. She glides away. For two minutes there is only the window sill and the large brass bed and the pile of clothes. She comes back to the bed and kicks the clothes under it with her foot. She paces three steps in back of the bed and out of range again. She does this twice. Then she sits on the window sill and stares into the camera. At different showings of the film, her eyes have reflected rage, fear, even humor. But her body remains understated, almost as if her movements have become anesthetized.

This morning I woke and the film was playing and she had three arms and her neck was moving in and out like a cobra and her pelvis was undulating forward . . . Now she stands and walks away, returning with Lockett. They sit on the bed. He looks tired and irritated. She caresses him, taking off his shirt, pushing him back on the bed. He covers his eyes with his forearm as she takes off his pants. Her mouth closes gently over his cock, and he moves slightly inside her. Fully aroused, he stands before her as she sinks backwards. He enters her. His plunges are short and abrupt. He watches her face but she has closed her eyes. He finally collapses on top of her. They lie on their backs and smoke, passing the cigarette back and forth. Meridith rubs out the cigarette on the wall and takes his face gently in her hands. She speaks to him, but Lockett shakes his head, as though unable to listen. He stares at her, angry. He dresses but stops once his pants are on, starting a motion to slap her. But his hand drops to his side. He leaves. A small vacant smile hovers at the corners of her mouth as she walks over to the window sill and empties a saucer underneath a fern that threatens to overflow.

Lockett has left but the loudspeaker continues. It offers instructions monotonously, as if the voice had become bored with itself: "Measure each other. Bow politely. Make a high sound and then a low sound. Bump against your clothes. Scream. Don't stop at the next intersection. Continue to flow but at the same time stop what you're doing. Don't calculate frequencies. Turn to the left . . ."

I don't listen. I feel rage. Rage at Lockett. Rage at his film. Rage at the brown blanket on top of the mattress and the blue one in front of the window. Rage at the deceptive cadences of the loudspeaker. Rage at the size of the room. Rage now, every few minutes, at the sound of footsteps in the hall. Rage at being somewhere else or not being somewhere else. Rage at what I've forgotten and what is taking its place. Rage at the words I let wander on.

I feel languid.

It's better to lie here just now and not draw attention to myself. Because there is a move pending. A move into the hall. Lockett plans to paint the room yellow, to place the mattress on top of a platform, to change the placements of the candles. It is being done for someone else; a prominent guest. I don't have to be told that. It is obvious. I am supposed to drag the mattress into the hall. I haven't been told that either, but I don't have to be told. When the loudspeaker is silent I can figure things out. I start to remember. It is gestures now, as I burrow for the last time under the brown blanket. (I don't want to start fast.) I'm lingering on the speed, fast or slow, of getting from one place to another, from the bathroom to the living room to the bedroom to the game room to the outside and back inside, to the bedroom.

I dragged the mattress into the hall. I have received no instructions. I will just lie here. The hall is dark. The mattress takes up the whole width of the hall, and anyone coming and going has to cross it. Eventually I will be told of another room, given a direction. Meanwhile my body can act as a kind of toll gate. I will make this space illumined for the people forced to cross over it. I can inhabit and furnish this space so that travelers will have a refuge, on the way to the bathroom or the way back from the bathroom. When the feet stop I can rub them and hold the ankles, reach up to the knees, to the inside of the thighs. I can touch them all, without exception, the mass of them, loosen them up, caress them without knowing what's above. I, too, can make a contribution. It is not enough to breathe in and out through the golden days . . . There is no loudspeaker out here. I am aware of the least noise, the softest tread. No one in the hall is so alert. I must be traveling very fast.

Lockett sits down. He is the first one. "I want to fly, man, to take off, to jump on the trampoline. I haven't managed to break out once. But now I have the key. I got it last night. *Now they will come to me.* I'm not going to let everyone into that cabinet. I traded the movie for the key. They plan to show it for money. All the cities of the West. I conned them so cool. They never knew what had happened until it was all over. The one they call Buffalo had it. He had to fall. He couldn't keep it up. Had it more than three weeks. We all knew he would fall. He was flipping, popping in any color that came along."

Whoever has the key to the cabinet located somewhere on the second floor has a certain prominence. As I have a certain prominence with my toll gate, which has become a kind of listening or trading post. Lockett wears a silver necklace around his neck and a small gold earring in his left ear. His hair looks even more curly. He affects a calmness, although I don't believe anything he says.

He winks. "I got to stay up. Those jackals are waiting for me. I got plenty to stay up on. When you're in control of all this you got to govern by a secret order and reveal it by degrees. They come at you anywhere, anytime. No game. I should be good for a week. Maybe longer. But I have something else going for me, sweet buddy. You want something you tell me."

"There are no stop signs here."

Lockett needs my mattress more than I need his cabinet. He has to have an oasis, a place to rest and hear what's happening. I encourage him. I roll my sock into a ball and let it roll out. Over the past two days the mattress has become crowded. Someone just sat down and put his legs against the wall. Although my eyes have gotten used to the dark, I try not to notice anyone too closely. Another man sat down and put his legs against the wall. This has begun to happen lately. There now exists an obstacle course on the way to the bathroom. A man has fallen asleep, his legs sliding down the wall and straightening out so that one misplaced step would cause a break.

The pillow becomes a sign of occupancy, that I am inhabiting this space. Without the pillow I might be mistaken for someone passing time. Perhaps I should nail the pillow to the wall. But I don't want to be too noticeable. I don't want to overextend myself, to advance too far. When I lose touch with the pillow, memories fly in and out of my head like small crippled birds. Something is mounting up. An operation of some sort. Possibly a general collapse. Just now, when the pillow slipped on the floor and I was holding on to a foot with one hand and rubbing a stomach with the other, I remembered the beach, how we joined hands in the rain and watched the breakers smash up the shore. It was a holiday. I had offered the octopus to neighbors as a present. It was something like that. I dragged the octopus out in the storm, and we each held a tentacle and twirled around and around. I am beginning to remember it was something like that. But I don't want to remember yet. It is too close. Not enough has happened. The pendulum still swings outward.

Meridith came, finally, in the middle of the night. She lay beside me on the mattress and threw a leg over my back. She was naked. I entered her slowly.

"Oh, Nog," she moaned. "I want to lie here and not move. I don't want any wild cards. Nothing sudden. I'm so tired. It's so much work, going over and over the plans. I'm hysterical. I like being inside you, or having you inside me. It's so hard to tell."

I told her about building the octopus and living with the Indians.

"I would like to make it with a tribe," she said.

I told her about walking over the Sierras in the late spring.

"Move now, a little," she said. "Don't tell me things. It gets in the way. In a circle, sort of, swing it around."

She suddenly wept.

I wanted to make her moan, but someone walked by, stumbling over me. I slipped out of her.

We listened to the toilet flush at the end of the hall.

I put my tongue in her ear. She smelled of lilacs. Her ear reminded me of the bathtub, and my tongue felt as if it were revolving inside a shell. If I could only get close enough, perhaps I could hear the sea. Aroused, I felt myself falling down the spirals of her ear. Her stomach became a pillow as I sucked away at her. But I want to sleep too. I want to fall away as she falls away. I raised myself and kissed her on the mouth.

"We aren't collaborating," she whispered. Again, the sound of flushing followed by steps. Someone has seated himself on the edge of the mattress, above my head. A hand caresses my brow. It is Lockett.

"Working out?" he asked. "Here, sweet buddy, this will get your heart to really pump."

There was a pop. Lockett held a capsule under my nose. I inhaled. It smelled like ether. I disappeared into the walls sliding over me, falling away, my back arching, and I came with a great spurt into the air. I slipped off, into sleep, but not before I heard another pop and saw the wraithlike form of Lockett, like a furious ghost, mount Meridith and ride away.

I have nailed the pillowcase to the wall, as a sign or a flag. I asked for and I received a hammer and nail. It's not safe here any more. And yet I am unable to creep out and establish some new space. Something has to happen, a new noise, a sense of something impending. Is it safe to say that? Nog, for instance, is not cruel enough. I've known that for the last few hours. If he is to continue melting into me, to help out, he must show more abandon. He must loosen up. He must become more perverse. I have shied away from cruelty for too long. It is a frozen need to be noticed that has led me to a series of tubs, shells, ears and rooms. At best, mushy beginnings. I have to get out of the hall. The mattress is beginning to stink. I cannot sustain not being clear about day or night, if the mattress really stinks. It's more comfortable at the end or beginning of a passageway. The middle is congested, full of plots and gropings. I could manage a story. A story might set a course. It's these moments before moving on when stories come flooding in. I've remarked on that before. It must be a way of calming myself, of not knowing what I'm doing. Stirring around does it, searching for a new place, a place to rest up, a place to wait for a beginning or an end. I don't know yet how to successfully cancel myself out. A place should do that, a warm place where there is no need, no thought even, of travel and stories. But I am always lured out. I stumbled to the Pacific to be at a new edge of the land. I thought it would help my breathing. Tiny waves plopped in as if they had been manufactured. Now there are no waves, and my breathing— But what about my breathing? It's still going on, in and out, in and out. I am losing the thread. I've done it again. I have to go back, or forward, to another edge. I must keep on forgetting. I must not remember the story I set out to tell. I must not betray myself. It is the only way. This doesn't help, setting it all down, discussing it, unraveling it and rolling it up like a dead tongue.

I took three short steps down the hall. Then three more short steps followed by two long ones. I am away. But I went back and sat on the filthy mattress and thought about passageways. I said that. But I never know exactly when I'm in a passageway or not. Should I even know about moving from one space to another? For instance: a dark path through the Douglas fir in Oregon led to a blacktopped road in Utah, to a winding alley in New York, to a long narrow cunt in Barcelona . . . no, it's the other way around. I don't trust the dim hint of light at the end of long tunnels, promises of events to come. It is enough to know the mattress is like a wrecked ship. It can't carry me. I unfurled the flag. Again I took three short steps down the hall, and again I have the suspicion I am away.

I tried the first door. It was on the right, as I moved toward the stairway. I opened without knocking. I am in no mood for knocking. The days and nights, the long vigil while afloat on the mattress, has left me wary of announcements. I am in touch with the thumpings and night beats of this house. But I feel no flush of arrogance. I feel no security. I went in the door and sat down, with my back to the wall. A girl lies on a red chaise lounge. She has long black hair, a sullen narrow face and a body disguised by a black satin evening gown. The light is blinding. There is an old wooden trunk partly covered with a red and black Navaho blanket. Other than the trunk and the chaise lounge, the room is empty. A small man in worn motorcycle boots, black chino pants and blue satin shirt sits on the edge of the trunk. He plays the "Stars and Stripes Forever" on an autoharp. He stops and addresses the girl, who has her eyes firmly closed. "I'm going to play this thing until you open your eyes. Come down from Portland to play with you, not at you, and I'm going to wing it over and over right through to the other side until you come off that couch and sit by me and we can see where we're at in terms of going on down there." He plays on. It is easy enough to imagine he is playing for me. I managed to pick up the outlines of their faces. A "sullen narrow face" is good enough. I'm not curious. The hard light on the floorboards impresses me more. Through the window I have seen a glimpse of the bridge. It is a relief to see a bridge, even though it made me shut my eyes and open them again when the bridge became a twisted and convoluted French horn. It is the shattering light. I have been a bridge once. I must not forget that. I threw myself across a small stream in the foothills, to be trampled over by a small child. And I have been played for. Meridith sang to me before the bath. That was weeks ago. I can't quite remember. That whole episode has faded. It's just as well. My mother played for me, or some mountainous shape, or rather, someone sang or crooned to me to keep me quiet, my mouth forever shut. But I don't want to go back there. It must be the shattering light. Memories become moldy. A slight turn and they become disgusting and rotten, oozing hope and lies.

"No more," the man said. He has stopped playing.

The girl sighed and opened her eyes.

"Best to get some speed in us," the man said. "Ride all day and most of the night. Get there before breakfast. Hot cakes, syrup, coffee, toast, eggs and bacon, maybe ham, marmalade and butter. Okay. Come down off the speed. Nicely spaced out. Start building. Build us a shack."

"Let's go to the kitchen, baby," the girl said.

"I'm in no hurry," the man said. "Feel like playing awhile."

"Or the park," the girl said. "We could try the park."

No one moves. I forget why I came into this room.

"The park," the man said finally.

"Play 'Blue Moon over Alabama,'" I said.

They are either ignoring me or they don't hear me.

I shut my eyes for several minutes and then opened them. Nothing has changed.

"My room," I said.

The man glanced at me. His face is round and wet, as if he has just emerged from under water.

"I'm tired of running in and out of rooms and finding the space taken," I said.

The man got up from the trunk and went over to the chaise lounge. He put his arm around the girl. They both look very young. "Nobody's room," he said.

"I have to paint the floor and the wall," I said.

"The floor and the walls don't need painting," the girl said. She looks older, almost instantly, and she wears heavy make-up around her eyes.

"My floors and walls are in constant need of re-touching," I said. I kept my eyes mostly on the floor.

But I can see the man advance towards me, holding his autoharp at one end, like an ax. He looks suddenly tired and middle-aged.

"I don't have anything to do with any room but this one," I said. "This is my room. I'm here, that's all. I didn't just wander in, to get my breath. I am the new guest." I tried to look into his eyes, but he avoided me.

But I saw them just the same. They are lined and red-rimmed. They are the eyes of an old man. I shut my own eyes.

I can hear the man squatting down beside me. "First you gentle them," he said quietly. "Then you turn them loose in the corral. You're going to like being in the corral. You'll be fed and you'll be able to hear what everyone else is doing. It takes getting used to. Like anything else. Now, just to put you at your ease, this room is definitely yours."

He strokes my clenched fist. He pried open my fingers one by one, but I managed to clench them again.

"Just sit," the girl said. I can feel her hand on my ankle. It should be the other way around.

"I don't attack spaces," I explained. "They attack me."

"Hand me the sugar," the man said.

"I don't have the sugar," the girl said. She giggled.

"You don't have the sugar?"

"I dropped the sugar."

"How long ago?"

"I don't know. Hours ago." Her hand tightens around my ankle.

"Where are you?" the man asked.

"In a large room," I said. "I've been trying to summon it up. To get a straight line going. The more I notice and count the cracks in the floor the more the days and weeks go by."

"I'm in the curl of a wave," the girl said. Her hand has abandoned my ankle. "I won't tell you the color.

The walls move. The walls of the wave. The walls are crumbling."

No one speaks. I still have my eyes closed. Now the autoharp plays "My Country, Tis of Thee." There is silence. I opened my eyes. There is another girl in the room. The light has faded. The girl is lying on the floor, her head against the trunk. I am too tired and the room is too dark to notice what she looks like. It doesn't matter. The girl with the sullen narrow face lies on the chaise lounge, her head on the man's lap. She is weeping. The man gazes out the window, perhaps at the lights on the bridge. It is a beautiful evening. There is no point in hiding. No one would notice. I shut my eyes. Then opened them. I haven't talked too much. I haven't disclosed too much. But that fear is behind me. I did get rid of the octopus. I gave it away. It has been a long move from Oregon to here. But it is time to move on. It is time to try another room.

I'm studying the cracks in another floor. I have been studying them too long. It is an abomination to keep traveling. It rots the mind. And yet what if I'm going somewhere, arriving at something? That would be unendurable. A while back it seemed the room was suddenly important and the breathers incidental. It was soothing for a brief moment. I would like to return there, without counting wooden wrinkles and informing on myself as each moment deserts me. It's definitely too soft, too primitive here. It's not possible to be shrill, to find a consistent sound to drown out all the other sounds. There is no such thing as a small noise. Everything comes together, ranging backwards and forwards, and then falls apart. Certainly nothing holds together here. A small boy sits in a corner and rips up a model airplane. The room is small and cramped, full of broken toys and a smell of talcum powder and urine. I should get everything up to this point, if I have to stuff it in and jam it on through, before the point disappears. I could invent another room. An empty room that I wandered in and out of without opposition . . . If I could say this again, begin again. It's not clear. But there is no time. Nothing remains the same. The boy cries and beats his fist on the floor . . . The cracks in the floor have widened. I need to find another space, a more restful space, a space I can strangle and tame long enough to hang on to. Then I'll come together in a mad rush. This room is obviously a sidetrack, and I don't need a sidetrack even if my main line hasn't come.

I crept into the hall. No one is about. There is the sound of distant singing or chanting. But I can ignore that. I tried the next door. It is locked. I'm grateful for that. I strolled down the hall. I went down the stairs, pausing on each one, as if to sniff the air. I have arrived at the second floor, not rested and calm but still, intact. I am hungry. I have not eaten regularly in the last few weeks. My system might be running down. I long to hunker down near a fire and get hot coffee in me and a buffalo steak. Then to slowly roll a cigarette, stretch and look up at the immense polluted sky. When a man gets to moving on he's got to have the right kind of vittles in his innards. There have been plates to scrape here, a candy bar or two, half a sandwich; sustenance for minor favors, a few gropings, a receptive posture, a lick or suck here and there. That kind of thing. I never pay attention . . . The plane has been ripped into pieces. All these blind maneuverings. He howls. I don't know how to howl. I have lost that. I might suddenly start. But no cheap scheme can save me now.

I left.

There is nowhere to go but down, down to the first floor, where I first came in. It was bound to happen. What goes up must come down. I have suspected all along I was returning to the kitchen. I am reeling along the hall, touching the walls. I turned to the right. I am in a food bin. The kitchen was either straight ahead or to the left. I was close but that might not count. I am on the floor, exhausted, my head leaning against a sack of potatoes. It is dark and cool, the wire mesh that covers the upper half of the wooden door diffusing and softening the light. The bin or closet, it is probably a large closet or pantry, is full. Carrots, onions, potatoes, pumpkins, cabbages, squash, bananas, apples and sacks of corn cover the floor. Cans and jars fill the shelves. It smells musty. A lock clicked. The profile of a man's head outlined against the wire mesh screen.

"Got you absolutely," a voice said, softly, gently. "The square on the lower left of the door slides open. You can shit in a pan and hand it through. There's a can opener on the wall. Eat anything. You want to change your head around, that's all right. You want to slow down, speed up, you want to go up, down, you want to have the walls fade in, fade out, you want to go inside, outside . . . that's all right. Rap on the door. You're off the kitchen. Someone will throw you something. You've been elected or got yourself elected. It doesn't matter. No one had their eye on you. But you were up to something in the hall. People were drifting up there. A shape to feel up. A place to hang out. There are bodies up there stuck on that mattress like flypaper. A man has to do his thing. Nobody here to deny that. But you went straight when you should have gone to the left. You missed the kitchen table. It happens. The hall was confusing. Tough to be messed up in the hall. I want to tell you the lock slipped in easy as vaseline just now. Nothing to it. No time like the present to slip a lock on someone. Your eyes will get used to the gloom. Keep them half closed, like you're peering down a gun barrel. There will be jobs for you, handing out stuff when it's asked for. Keep yourself occupied. Exercise. Deep breathing never hurts, push-ups, swing the neck around, touch your toes if you have room, isometric stuff, recite to yourself, that kind of thing. Other people have grooved in there. But you're doing fine. No need to tell you anything. I'm doing fine, and there isn't any need to tell me anything."

The profile disappeared.

A delicate moment, when the line draws taut, when the lurching from wall to wall suddenly ends. I will miss the complaining and whining . . . Where do these words come from? There's no need for them now. But they dribble on. Nog, of course, can become clearer. Or dropped. Or simply forgotten. He hasn't helped out yet. He's dumber than I once thought. The way time continually eludes Nog when he's confronted with a soft unexplored space is unforgivable. No, that's me. I have to watch that . . . To get over the expanse, from the first Douglas fir to the luncheonette, to dissolve the distance, cadence must be counted. Lists and comparisons must be made, the body checked out, everything secure in its place, temperature taken, blood flowing, urine and stools regular . . . In this vast space among the potatoes and corn, a schedule must be kept. Nothing else for it . . . I will peer around from time to time, to lessen the anxiety of waiting for a schedule to be formed . . . It is moist. The vegetables will become an envelope, an extension of my skin. I will grow avocado plants. Fungus will appear between my toes. Obviously I'm in a huge mouth or a section of a dome or skull. That I might be crouched in an oversized cunt never occurred to me. Let it be a mouth, a mouth stuffed with undigested food. The food has been stolen. I have been stolen. They're talking it over in the kitchen. I can hear mumbling voices and the scrape of silverware on dishes . . . The sack of potatoes is crouched in the back, against the wall. Sly, to protect themselves against exposure. We could all be in a boxcar. A boxcar hurtling across the Southwest towards a concentration camp . . . No, I can't manage that, can't get around to that. It's a mouth. Anyone's mouth. That's the way I have been headed, more towards the mouth than any other opening. I see that clearly. If I can only squeeze myself into a small ball, like a piece of bread crushed and rounded between thumb and forefinger . . . That's a start . . . Then to drop down the throat, into the miles and miles of intestines. To be digested and swirl out the other end. But I have to get sucked into it. It takes relaxation. You're either being chewed or you're not being chewed. If that is true, if I am being swallowed, then this black orifice might be where it all ends. If I only believed that. Just for a moment. If I only believed a line finally stops, that the walls of the terminal, like inflated rubber, can be punctured enough to deflate. But a long hiss is too much to hope for.

I fell asleep, hours or days ago. There is no sound from the kitchen. I awoke slowly, just now, but then came on with a rush, attempting a crouch, the beginnings of a leap, ready to assail, to attack this space. But there is no room for that. I rearranged the cans on the shelves and the vegetables and fruit on the floor. Words like vegetables run into and climb on top of each other. No matter. There is work to do. It is enough to open a can of tuna fish, not necessarily to eat it. An icebox throbs. A chair scrapes. Someone is out there, sitting at the table. It's too far away to hear if there is more than one. I heard a deep sigh.

A scratch on the wire mesh screen. It's too dark to distinguish a profile. I'm trying to quiet myself, to keep my muscles from tensing.

I crawled to the door.

I'm waiting by the door.

I've been in tight places before. A railroad station. A back seat. A thicket. A lap. A cabin. A hotel room. Only exteriors wrapped around the meat. As for events, they come and go . . .

"I know you're in there." It is a girl's whisper. "Everyone says you're in there. I suppose it doesn't matter whether you're in there or not. But I think you're in there. You can hand something out if you want, through your little hole . . . I've been sitting in the kitchen. It's hardly ever empty, even at three in the morning. It's after four now. You have to wait just to sit alone . . . Would you like anything? But why should I give you anything? I've never seen you. You've probably never seen me. Hank felt you up though. It was in the yellow room. Or maybe in the bath. I get confused. Hank tells me everything, but I forget. I even forget why I came here. But I want to tell you. I have to tell somebody. I remembered you were in the food bin. I remembered the name. Nog. Your name has started to go around. They're talking about it. I don't know what they say. I don't even know what I'm saying . . . Hank has disappeared. He didn't say anything to anyone. People come and go here all the time. No one keeps track . . . I'm not from around here. I came up by bus. I didn't know it wasn't a regular bus. Hank was driving . . . What I'm trying to get at is . . . I don't know. Do you like to grab someone when they come along? I'm not too old. I like it when someone just takes me. I wish I could tell you all the things I think. I'm going to come back. No, scratch that. I had to come down once. I was sitting in the kitchen, that's all. But I'll bet you're not even in there . . . I'm so down. I can't take it any more. I don't know what's going into me or going out of me."

I can hear her crying. She dropped a blue sneaker with a plastic bag of white pills in through the hole.

"I had to work up to it. At first I didn't think I was going to give you anything. I didn't even tell you what was on my mind . . . I'm upstairs at the end of the hall, if you get upstairs again. I'll lie here for a few minutes in case you want to say anything or let me know you're in there. I'll bet you aren't even in there."

I passed an open can of tuna fish through the hole.

That was days ago. There have been many scratches on the wire mesh screen. Goods have been passed back and forth. I have tee shirts, drawings, candles, poems, a comic book, toys and photographs. I pass out whatever I lay my hand on. I don't give out any information. I have yet to talk. I can almost smell another presence in here, fetid and languid. If I speak, it might go away. I keep a list of the goods and voices that come through the hole and wire mesh screen. They are increasing in amount and intensity. There are other voices, more seductive, disconnected voices, voices in the kitchen or traveling up and down the hall, but it is enough now to open up to the voices connected with profiles. There have been sixteen voices, not counting those voices that have repeated themselves. There has been one voice that has come through the screen over thirty times. I list each voice for weight, density, force and distance. Talking now is number seventeen: heavy, like a flounder sinker caught in the throat, massive but only on top, little force and range between words. I listen to every third or fourth word. It has begun to seem like one voice, all the voices, a huge voice, sobbing and laughing, complaining and praising itself. The voice doesn't go backward or forward. It doesn't know what it wants: "My chin don't track with the rest of my face . . . Leadville to Carmel to Santa Fe. I'm close to that word 'bravado.' You know what I mean . . . Learn the Indian way and forget the rest of it . . . I know where *you're* at, Nog. Wild old mountain man . . . I never look to anyone for food or shelter, but I'll be waiting for you when you make your move . . . We're not going to let any of them in any more. Ever."

A clenched hand enters the hole. It remains clenched for several minutes. A key slowly drops through the fingers. It must be the key to the cabinet. I prefer to think it is the key to the cabinet. How many keys can there be around here? Several, no doubt. But even so, it is the key to the cabinet. I had my hand around a potato, but I didn't pass it out. I shoved the key into the potato and put the potato into the sack. I am a repository, I suppose. The dark wet hole where everything finds its way sooner or later. I remain near the entrance, handling goods as they are shoved in, listening and nodding. I have been slowly dissolving into this cavity. That is a change. A vegetable roundness anyway. I am grateful for that. If I could find some better way to repeat my presence so as to cancel out its effect, to make an offering of that, to this space. If nothing else works, I can wait for days, weeks if necessary, when the key will become huge and soft by its absence, and then hand it out, to renew the ritual they so depend on. I could do that.

Hours or perhaps a day after the key had been deposited, I let myself kneel forward, in supplication, towards the hole. Someone is out there. But instead of a voice, the latch slid open and the door was flung open. Lockett and Meridith stand before me.

"It's all over," Lockett said. "We got to get out."

He is dressed in boots, blue jeans and a windbreaker. He has a pack on his back. Meridith wears a blue cotton dress and an orange sweater. The sudden light blinded me. I shrank back.

"I'm staying," I said.

Lockett walked forward, into my space. I pushed a sack of potatoes in his way, but he knocked it aside. I must be moving on.

"No place for you," I said. I tried to shout, to show my alarm, but my voice is only a whisper, perhaps even a plea.

Lockett took a quick step and hit me over the head with a weighted sock.

RECOLLECT a '41 Ford rode me out of Wichita. Clear across four states before she humped another car. Killed a man. Broke my arm in two places. Made a splint out of the jack and kept going straight into the sun. Never was one to look back . . ."

I am in the back seat of a car. Lockett is talking, his voice somehow a refuge. One low note over and over. I have a craving for Nog, for the calm light streaming out of his chest. I am becoming Nog, I am Nog, except that he slips away. He has slipped away.

Meridith leans her head on Lockett's shoulder. Her fingers play absently with his ear.

"Stole me a Chevy, baby. Drove that Chevy clear to Utah. Never was partial to Chevies. Now I loved that '41 Ford. But it was a Packard got me put away. Locked up for three years. I had the wires crossed and was ready to roll when they slipped up. That barrel pressed up against my skull and that voice saying, 'Where you goin, boy?'"

My breath gushes out of me as if in an endless exhale. The house has been a long hysterical inhale. A place to start. Let it be that. The sky is through the window. The seat is of cracked brown leather. My head throbs. But the clouds move. They move slowly and ponderously from the window next to me to the front-seat window. They don't come back, but others have replaced them. There are always others. A tree leans towards the window. The tree lasts several thoughts or sounds. It is still there. But it has stopped. Lockett's voice is no longer a refuge, and we aren't moving after all. Lockett turned and Meridith's fingers fell from his ear.

"Figured you to be in need of a stop."

There is no need for memories, although I could use a list. But not now. Memories are killing. There is no need to go over the long solitary trek from the mountains to the sea, a clean yellow light streaming from my chest. No need to remind myself of the riot in the supermarket, the enclosure in the house. I have lost more of a direction than that. It is now erosion of whole houses, the invasion of hide-outs pregnant with maps and plans.

"Whoever you were before coming aboard, you're purely different now. You'll drop out like a man or know the reason why." Lockett grinned. His eyes are ferocious with love and compassion.

I am slower, more driven to silence, since that pitiful time on the beach, since the octopus, since I lied about the octopus. My head throbs, for one thing. The outlines of profiles are grayer. They arrive and depart faster, with less warning. Nothing is defined. I haven't been interrupted. But that is terrifying. There is only a dull reaching out now, for forms now vanished, my arms, call them tentacles, barely touching anything, content to feel the front seat, the bump on my forehead. There must have been an embrace, back there, in the house, in the food bin, half an embrace, the other half left inside the potato. I was bending over the potato, that is clear enough, inserting myself in its wound, slowly moving my cock up and down, and the door was flung open. That was it. The door was flung open and I couldn't handle the surprise.

The front door opened and slammed. Meridith peers in the right rear window, Lockett the left.

"You're awake," Meridith whispers shyly. Her long blond hair is twisted into braids, one of which she tugs absently.

"Recollect I had my first piece in a Packard," Lockett said. "Almost broke my back, but she was crazy for me."

Lockett pulls his mouth down with his thumb and forefinger. He wrinkles his nose and widens his eyes. There is a heavy white film on his eyelids. Perhaps he is trying to make me laugh. "Seems like they almost had you in there," he said.

"Nobody had me."

"He doesn't need entertaining," Meridith said.

Their heads have disappeared.

I pulled my own head up to the window and saw them duck behind a privet hedge. It is too overwhelming to climb out of a back seat, into an open space, or perhaps a lack of space. You can never be too careful. The car is stationed either in front of a large park or at the edge of a wilderness. The sky is still above it all. I sank back. I am denying myself a gallop. It has been too long since I've dashed through a decent amount of space. I need the run, my arms pumping, my nostrils flaring, my tongue hanging out, my heart pounding, my eyes rolling up at the hideous clouds.

I did climb out of the back seat and with a shout rush to the edge of the privet hedge. It was a long enough run, nearly two hundred feet. I sank to the ground after I had staggered past the first hedge. I shut my eyes. I don't want to see too much. It is more than enough to lie here on the grass, to smell and feel the grass beneath me. If I can somehow build up enough smells, enough of a sense of the sky pushing me down, holding me down, then my eyes will open of themselves. Lockett laughed. I sang out, suddenly ecstatic, "Snap your fingers, baby, and I'll come running. That's the truth . . ." More giggles. I opened my eyes, easily, as if they opened by themselves. But the earth turns too fast. I focused on the branches of a tree, and then taking my time, I looked at Meridith, who is straddling a tombstone and smelling a bunch of daisies. We must be in a graveyard. There are flowers at her feet. Lockett is on his knees, gathering three bouquets together.

"After this job we'll head south and to the east a bit. I know a place."

I am more relaxed, knowing that there is, after all, a place, that we are heading for a definite place.

Lockett and Meridith pulled me to my feet. They escorted me to the car, an old Chrysler airflow. Lockett threw the bouquets over the dashboard, and we drove off. We drove into the center of the city. We drove in silence. I lay lengthwise on the back seat and watched roofs and the tops of trees go by. There is still the sky. We pulled into a parking lot adjoining a hospital.

"Check the MD cars," Lockett said. "If anyone stops you, you're visiting a relative. You're looking for your car."

Lockett handed us each a bouquet, and we looked for cars that had MD on their license plates. I'm not really looking. They must have told me what to look for, but I have forgotten. Lockett and Meridith were unable to find anything. We went up the steps and into the hospital. Lockett seems to know where he wants to go. We followed him into the In Patients waiting room and sat down on a bench. An ancient Negro woman with dyed blue hair sits behind us. Her arm is in a sling, and there is matted blood over one eye. She smiles and hums to herself. Lockett rolls a cigarette.

"Nothing for it but to check the rooms," he said.

"Are we looking for someone?" I asked.

"If you want to look for someone, you go ahead and look for someone. But be back here in thirty minutes."

Meridith giggled.

They left . . . I don't know how much time has elapsed. Long enough to get used to sinking down on the bench, to get accustomed to being a patient. I forget now why I'm here and why I'm not being received, why the nurse passes me in favor of the Negro lady. But I do remember that we are looking for someone. I have to at least take a look around. I have to do my part.

I walked down the corridor and up a flight of stairs. I am in another corridor. The walls aren't sliding in. I'm moving straight ahead. I am in another corridor. The turn was confusing, but I am still going forward. A nurse passes. I reached out, but she didn't respond. She too must be involved in gliding straight ahead. A door is open. I walked in. An old man lies on a bed, propped up by pillows. His head is enormous, seeming to float above the rest of his body like a balloon. His pale blue eyes are small but very brilliant. His mouth moves in and out like the suckings of a goldfish. There is a force inside him; perhaps a pump planted there, drawing everything inside, stretching his skin and hollowing out his eye sockets. Except for that peculiar motion with his lips and his staring eyes, he might be dead. There are yellow roses on a bedside table in a white porcelain vase. I contributed my bouquet to the vase and placed a rose in my buttonhole. I pulled a chair up to the bed and sat down. I smiled at him, trying to make my lips rigid and friendly. It is a relief to be sitting in a chair in a clean white room. I would like to prolong it as long as possible. Blood drips into his arm from a hose attached to a bottle on a stand. I patted the bottle. There is nothing wasted in this room, nothing irrelevant, except perhaps for a white Stetson on top of the dresser. I put the Stetson in the top drawer of the dresser and sat down again. I lifted up the brown blanket and tickled the bottom of a wrinkled foot. He dribbles at the mouth and lowers his eyes. He has an egg-shaped head, so huge and barren, the kind of skull anyone would be proud to have on a night table or desk.

"I'm fond of bones," I said, "especially when they have a good bleach to them. I used to have a sheep's skull myself. Polished it and hung it from a chain over my bed. Day and night for weeks. That was in New York. I needed the kind of focus a skull can give you. I suppose I was trying to keep from moving on. But I left. I wandered across the country. My friends took to calling me Nog. But I'm not in here to give away my secrets. I just want to pass the time for ten minutes. A lovely room."

I peered closer and tried to look fully into his eyes, but he has managed to close them. His lips have stopped moving. At the same time my foot has fallen asleep. I jumped up and down to get my circulation going. He opened his eyes. His lips are moving furiously.

I leaned my head down to his mouth.

"Easy, General," I said. "There's nothing more to do. Everything has been built, everything said, everything ruined. They even control the weather. There's no place to go. You cross the country and keep looking onward and you can only get into trouble. You got yourself a decent space. Seventy-five inches by thirty-five, give or take a few. You've got it made. They bring food to you, take it away, bedpans in and out, flowers on the table, draw and raise the shades, wake you and put you out. They even turn the television on and off. No sense to agitate until they drop you into an even smaller, more final space. Then holler all you want."

I went to the dresser and took out the Stetson. I put it on and stood at attention in front of the bed. The Stetson is several sizes too big. He is trying to speak again. I took off the Stetson and put my ear next to his flapping lips.

"Lit a shuck . . . cork boots . . . two hundred acres soy beans . . . a deal . . . center stock. . . Sweet Alice Hills . . ."

His lips are still moving, but his voice has faded.

A nurse walked in.

"Who gave you permission to be here?" she asked. She is large-boned and middle-aged. Her graying hair is tied behind her in a neat bun. Her dress crackles when she moves.

"You have to have permission to be kin of someone?" I rose from the chair. "This old man knew how to put one foot in front of the other. He walked across the Sierras and mapped most of the Northwest. Lived alone in a shack in British Columbia. Had a broken leg in the Sweet Alice Hills and dragged himself forty miles before he passed out in a field of soy beans. Half dead, he was washed away by a flash flood, his deer-hide shirt torn off his back, his six-shooter lost forever. A half-breed Kiowa found him and left him in a hut full of stolen goods. Been up the river and over the mountain, that old man. Never one to ask for anything. Made himself a rubber octopus and traveled through the West with it, charging kids a dime and grownups a quarter. He made out. Carved his own space with his own hands. Traded his goods, grew his crops, raised his kids and never signed his name to anything. Kin comes over a thousand miles to share his last breath with him and you order him out. Seems whenever I get somewhere with a chair and clean white walls, I get ordered out."

My voice had risen. I placed my Stetson on my head and edged toward the door, the Stetson falling over my eyes.

"He came clear across the country and there's nowhere else to go. You come in and ask about permission. What kind of control freak are you? He's choking to death. Can't you see that? He has no idea why he's in this room, doesn't even remember why he's here or know if he's ever getting out."

"Your first time, dear?" she asked softly.

"Last time. The last time is the one that gets you because it leads right into the first time. Nowhere to go. But you go on anyway. The more you go on the more you stop thinking about going on, because you're thinking about it all the time. Everything backs up. It gnaws here on the edge, looking back in order not to look forward."

"He's not feeling any pain," she reassured me.

I looked over at the bed. The general was sleeping peacefully.

I backed out the door. I went down the corridor and down the stairs to the In Patients waiting room. I sat down on a bench and made a list of mountains I have been on or thought I might have been on: Mount Olive, Mount Washington, Mount Snow, Mount Baldy, Mount Frazier, Mount Crystal, Mount Wolf, Mount Cheney, Mount Karabakh, Mount Kanchenjunga, Mount Chimborazo, Mount Cotopaxi, Mount Monadnock and Mount Ruwenzori. I was listing ranges of mountains when Lockett and Meridith sprinted past. I followed them out the door and into the car.

Lockett threw a black doctor's bag next to me on the back seat. He told me to throw it on the floor. He drove down several side streets and then doubled back. Then he drove out of the city. After several hours he pulled off the side of the road into a picnic area.

We got out of the car and sat down on one of the wooden benches. There are no other people. The area is peaceful, with shaded trees and the dull hum of cars from the highway. Lockett went over to the car and came back with the doctor's bag. He carried it behind a tree. Meridith and I followed. He spread the contents of the bag on the ground.

"Meridith snatched it," Lockett said. "It was on a chair outside an office."

He reached slowly into the bag and withdrew three tongue depressors. He spread them on the ground a few inches from each other. Then he pulled out a thermometer and a vial of tranquilizers. He arranged the thermometer and tranquilizers to the right and left of the tongue depressors, creating the upper half of a star. He shut his eyes, his hands groping in the bag before emerging with clenched fingers. The fingers slowly opened, exposing a small vial in his palm.

"Morphine," Meridith whispered.

"Morphine," Lockett added.

The vial was placed into the center of the star. Rapidly he withdrew Band-Aids, gauze, an ear syringe, a regular syringe with a box of needles, more tranquilizers, a stethoscope and a box of Q-tips. The star was completed.

"A start," Lockett said. "Find us a place and build. Which don't mean there is no place, you understand."

Meridith dropped a small black stone in the bag. Then she took a button off her dress and dropped that in.

"Nog," Lockett commanded.

"No," I said.

"You're in," Meridith said.

I backed away. "The roots of the tree." I pointed to a huge oak whose roots are exposed and are reaching away from the trunk, creating a small hollow. I'm unable to explain.

Lockett drew a switchblade from his boot. He walked towards me, snapping it open. His eyes are steady and vacant. He holds the knife a few inches from my throat. With a swift motion he raised the knife and cut a small triangle from the brim of the Stetson. He handed me the triangle. I dropped it into the bag. He cut a small circle from the center of his shirt and dropped the circle into the bag. He snapped the bag shut and carried it over to the car.

We drove south into heavily wooded hills that gradually grew higher. We left the highway and drove on a winding blacktop and then turned off into a small dirt road. We drove into gathering darkness, and the light and the road ended at the same time.

Lockett opened the trunk and took out two army packs. We are surrounded by trees, but I sense peaks above us. Lockett handed one pack to me and one to Meridith. My pack is heavy, being full of canned food. Lockett carries the black bag and several dark green blankets. He plunges into the woods.

There might be a path. Specifics drift away from me. There seems to be a series of shifting wooded corridors becoming smaller and smaller. I stumbled behind Meridith. Mosquitoes sting my exposed skin. My clothes are thin and offer little protection. I focused on Meridith's heels and then, gaining courage, on her ankles. She wears faded blue sneakers with no socks. I lurched a step closer. There is something about the methodical way she picks up her foot and sets it down that sends my heart thumping, my mouth dry, no exaggeration, there is something gay and insane about following her because it has nothing to do with her. There have been other ankles, to be sure, other feet, plodding on in front of me, toes curled in, planted in the sand. On the beach at Biarritz, Acapulco, Corfu. No, that's not it. I'm following. I followed for hours, branches bent forward by Meridith's passage whipping my face and body. I am content to follow. When we stumbled into a small clearing I collapsed next to Meridith's feet as she sank to the ground.

The clearing reaches back from a small river. I can hear the river moaning quietly. The clearing is the size of a waiting room in a provincial railroad station. Redwood trees press around us. Above, there are cold stars. Lockett spread the blankets on the ground. Then he gathered sticks for a fire. Meridith took out cooking utensils from her pack. She cooks two cans of chili and beans and coffee. No one has spoken since we examined the black bag, making Lockett's voice sound distant and strained.

"Found me this place a few years back. Came out to kick a habit. Figured I could keep busy, trap a few animals, build me a shack. Never happened. First night out saw a woman come out of them trees with about seven or eight arms on her. She was grinning and reaching out and I backed up so fast I landed on the fire. Almost burned the habit out of me. Next few weeks I rolled on the ground, and plenty of times I set off to go back. That woman always blocked the way. I had to get hold of a plan to keep from flipping. Been thinking of that plan ever since. Got me some goods cached back in the trees."

Lockett walked out of the light. I took off my clothes and stretched out on a blanket. No one can see me, unless Lockett has circled around and now stares at me from the rear. Meridith is on the other side of the fire. I'm afraid to let go of this moment, in this clearing, this particular moment. That recent trip, the transition from back there, in the house, to this moment, this clearing, has dissolved some part of me. I am diminished as well as expanded. But now there is a clearing. There are the trees and the cold stars. There is the smell of the earth and the moaning of the river. I want to back up, not to let a memory slip into this clearing, to push it all back, to keep locked in, to curl my toes, in this clearing, never mind the rest, and when it ends, when I have to rush out again, the momentum might be desperate enough to wrap myself finally around myself. But the night is too gentle, and the pressure hisses out of me. I can't hold it. I am in the middle of a soft insidious hush, aware only that something is impending, that nothing has been pushed backward or forward, that I am in the middle of a clearing, that what is impending is a mosquito and the hard bark of Lockett's laugh and the stars too far away.

I walked to the river. I took off a shoe and stuck a foot in. The water is warm and caressing. It pulls at me, at my foot, at the lower part of my leg, at my thigh, at my balls. I replaced my boot and walked back to the fire. Then I walked to the river. I took off my other boot and put that foot and leg into the water. The water laps and caresses me once more. I replaced my boot and walked back to the fire. I stood before the fire until my boot began to burn. Then I walked back to the river. I'm standing in the soft mud. I heard a croak several feet to the left. I'm not interested in what happens several feet to the left. My boots are covered with mud. The dark form of a bird sweeps low over the water. I walked to the fire. I'm sitting with my back to the fire. My back has become too hot and I walked around the fire, stepping over Meridith curled up on a blanket. I walked to the edge of the clearing and bent down on my knees in front of a redwood. The trunk is several feet around. I am unable to see the branches above me. I will take them for granted. A weight pulls my forehead down, almost to the ground.

I must be prostrating myself. A stream of letters pours out of my head into a small golden bowl. It doesn't matter that I've thrown up. I backed away from the redwood tree and lay down on my blanket. I lay on my back and then on my stomach and then on my back. A huge hand moves over the shadows cast by the fire. Meridith is jerking off. I pulled my blanket close to her. Her dress is pulled over her waist and she is staring at the stars.

"Why must we keep discovering each other?" she asked.

She moaned and threw a leg over my waist.

"I do my jerking off in the city," I said. "I'm all business out here. In the city I take warm baths and hang around. I pull down the shades and get myself squarely in the middle of the mattress. The least arbitrary movement does me in. It's enough to listen. Out here there's enough to do, what with reading signs and checking out every shift in the wind, every bent twig and leaf."

Her body slid next to mine. I clutched at it, afraid that it might roll away.

"I hope I can lose weight out here," Meridith said. "I know he's fixing to move on. Every time I get my body tone up, we move on. It's been this way for years, if not with him then with someone else. I get so tired. I thought the last time we were located for good. Then he grabs me and we're out the door."

I slipped my cock inside her.

"Did you notice any labels on the cans?" she asked. She bit my neck. She has begun to move slightly. "Those labels are almost completely worn off, those cans are so old and that chili was the worst I ever had."

"It's a web out here," I said. "Everything is joined. Make one wrong move and you'll start a forest fire or cause the collapse of some animal."

I thrust suddenly at her and she has become a hot river. I floated down her, rolling over and over like a submerged log. She moves and rolls with me and we moan together.

Over her shoulder I can see Lockett walk slowly out of the woods. He is dragging a deflated yellow rubber boat.

We stopped, my cock still rigid inside her.

"The rest of the goods didn't last," Lockett said. He dropped the yellow boat and took off his clothes. He stands with his back to the fire, staring towards the river. "Had a hassle finding where I hid the goods. Thought it was back to the west, but it was more to the east. Bowie knife still good. Dynamite wasted."

He lay down on the other side of Meridith, facing her back. Meridith leans forward, throwing a leg over my waist. I shifted deeper inside her. Lockett rubbed his hands up and down Meridith's back.

"Down there is the desert," he said. "The Agua Dulce Mountains. Might be off a bit, but we'll still be north of the desert when we get to where we're going. We'll float down."

With a long sigh he urged himself into the rear of Meridith. I let him get going before I began again. Meridith has her eyes shut. She breathes heavily. There are three or more hands on my chest. Lockett's breathing has grown louder and dominates every other sound. My own tentative breaths have grown more agitated. We are all groaning together. Meridith screamed. She pulled my hair and I saw the stars like silver bursts of rifle fire. I managed to hold on. I can feel somewhere in the deep background Lockett's own efforts for survival. Meridith finally came with a long shuddering spasm followed closely by Lockett, whose arms and legs wrap over Meridith in his final embrace. I plunge on alone. It is a time to ruminate. A force is building inside me. I feel the hint of something, a line broken, another line joined, a few extra breaths seized. I am about to break away from all the weights behind me and create new weights. It is becoming clearer, the line from where it begins to where it is going, but I suddenly came.

I woke before the others. The fire has died to a few coals and it is very dark. It's not any easier after a short nap. There are no memories to help out. Somewhere wild turkeys call sweetly on the Big Fork. But that was Nog. I hear nothing. But then, I too have crawled through woods with a pack on my back to a small clearing by a river. Lockett stirs. I heard him get up and go over to the edge of the clearing. He is blowing up the rubber boat. In April, I have smelled dogwood above Ten Foot Orchard. I want to sleep. But I dressed and built up the fire. Meridith woke and went into the woods to pee. She came back and sleepily started the coffee. We are breaking camp. Either that or we are getting ourselves set for a long stay. But air is being blown into a rubber boat.

Lockett returned. We drank coffee.

Lockett's movements are more defined. He speaks

slower, as if from far away. He touches objects with reverence. He holds his empty coffee cup in both hands and licks slowly around the rim. Only when his tongue has completed two full circles around the rim does it return to his mouth. His hands linger on a boot. He rubs the leather sides. He is still naked. Meridith and I are both dressed, and that fact seems to have drawn us closer together. In any case, she has gripped my hand with hers. We watch Lockett. He stands and spreads his arms. He bends forward and picks up his shirt. In a loose motion he twists it under his crotch and around his waist. He smiles. Then he digs a hole with his bowie knife. He puts the pants into the hole and covers them with dirt. He slips the bowie knife into the shirt around his waist and squats by the fire. Then he puts on his boots.

"Time to move," he said. "When we get there the sun will be up and we'll walk in."

"He's on something," Meridith whispered to me.

All-knowing compassion spreads loosely over Lockett's face. He advances towards us, holding out his emaciated arms. He encircles us, drawing us to him. His breath is heavy and rancid. His skin is like sandpaper. "We're moving out," he said, releasing us.

Meridith and I put on our packs. Lockett carried the three blankets and the black bag down to the river. Then he went back and dragged down the rubber boat. It looks round and bulbous. Lockett threw in the blankets and carefully put the black bag on top of them. He waded into the river and splashed water on his face. He holds the side of the boat and motions for Meridith to get in. She shakes her head and steps backwards. I'm holding her hand. Lockett silently regards us. Finally he shrugged and climbed into the boat. He was preparing to shove off when Meridith waded into the river and hauled herself over the edge of the boat. She sits timidly on the side, holding on with both hands. She reached out a hand for me. I feel myself being drawn forward. Too much has happened not to go on now. I slipped in the mud but managed to throw myself over the side. I'm sitting opposite Meridith. I have remembered my Stetson and pulled it firmly over my eyes. But Meridith pushed it back. Lockett sits in the bottom of the boat, holding the black bag and leaning his head against Meridith's thighs. Nothing happened. Then the boat began to slowly slip away.

I heard myself close my eyes, then open them. We are away now, moving faster, turning around and around, bumping into rocks and sliding off. We are in the middle of the river, moving quietly. I can't see the sides of the river. There is only the dark water and a gathering coolness. Now there is a rushing sound of water over rocks. We bumped hard and spun around twice. I'm gripping the sides of the boat, squeezing into the rubber. Meridith has sunk to the bottom. She holds my legs. The darkness is heavier, and I can feel the presence of high canyons on either side. We are going faster. There is the sound of rapids now. I put a foot on Meridith's stomach. It doesn't help. A roar envelops us. We are swept backwards over a series of jagged rapids. White water surrounds us. There is nothing to hold on to. Now a quiet stretch. It is lighter. I can see the vague shape of a large animal standing in the water, his head raised, looking at us. Faster now and there is a roar again. It isn't possible to speak. My stomach is clenched, my mouth dry. There is a hiss near my hand. It is a leak. I put my finger over it. Then I took it off and then I put it on again. I finally took it off altogether. There are other hisses now, and there is no use bothering. We are sinking lower. I have been swimming at night before, huge waves rolling me over and over. It is better not to resist. In the storm at the beach the undertow had reached out for me. I had offered the octopus instead. It was accepted. We are in calm water. The river has widened. We are sinking slowly. There is water now in the bottom of the boat, and Meridith and Lockett are sitting on the sides. Lockett either doesn't notice or care. He scans the shore.

"Soon now," he mutters.

The boat is half full of water. Lockett holds the bag and a pack in his arms. Meridith holds the rest of the goods. I paddle towards the shore. We did, in fact, reach the shore, although we had to wade a few feet.

Lockett sank his knife into the side of the boat, leaving it to sink to the bottom of the river.

Meridith and I put on our packs. Lockett carries the bag and the blankets. He led us rapidly away from the river. We climbed a series of sharp serrated ridges, slipping several times on the rocky ground. We are climbing steadily. He seems to know where he's going, although there is no hint of a path. It is becoming lighter. We move without stopping, breathing hard. It doesn't help to watch Meridith's ankle. I went over a list of mountains, adding a few and subtracting a few. We have passed cactus and deep washes. Finally, on top of a steep rocky bluff, Lockett stopped. Below us, in the distance, glows a faint light. We sat and watched the dawn reveal the valley and the town. There is a street with four or five wooden buildings facing each other. In back, there looms the hump of a steep mountain. The narrow rugged valley is full of brutal black shadows. Nothing moves. There is no sound.

"This is where Meridith and I go it alone," Lockett said.

I have forgotten how to object.

"You got the blankets and the packs. That's enough for a start. Build some kind of a wickiup near that boulder over there. This isn't a bad ledge. You can make out here. Everything will develop now. You'll be hearing from us or we'll be hearing from you."

They stood up. I'm still sitting, clutching the bag. It is comforting. They are moving off the ledge. I can hear rocks sliding. I caught one glimpse of them, walking hand and hand, before they disappeared in a gully at the beginning of the valley.

THERE are no trees. The town is further away than before, across a deep web of arroyos. I have been sleeping. It is late afternoon. There are eight or nine houses in the town, and a dirt road winds down from the mountain into the town. Two houses appear to have fallen in on themselves. There are three tepees in back of the town, halfway up the mountain. In back of the tepees are old machines, and in back of the machines are dark shadows which might be caves or excavations. I put my fist in front of my face but I can still see. It is very hot. The sky is too huge. I crawled to the rear of the ledge to hide the black bag under a rock. A rattlesnake slowly raised its head. I threw the bag at him and ran to the edge of the ledge. I'm there now. In back of the ledge are twisted saw-toothed ridges. There must be a trail that Lockett followed. But I have lost the knack of recognizing a trail. Meridith and Lockett know I'm out here. Unless they've forgotten. They might have told someone I'm out here. But it isn't like them to walk into a town and hand out information. They might have walked through the town without stopping and gone over the mountain. There might be a city over the mountain, or a ball park, or an airplane factory . . . There is no noise in the whole blown and eroded valley. I have to turn to the rear, to the small cavity in back of the ledge. From that hole I can look safely out at the ledge. I can sit low enough so that I won't see the valley or the town. I can handle the mountain. I have a list of mountains to help out. The ledge needs smoothing out. There are rocks to move or think about moving and measurements to be paced out. There is a smaller, less exposed ledge a few hundred feet down, but it doesn't have the beginnings of a cave. I need the beginnings of a cave. I must arrange the cans of food in alphabetical order and build protection from the sun. I must pace backwards and forwards. Never mind the snake. There never was a snake. I must find water. I must manage a few memories, now that the sky is so huge. I must burrow into rock, and to do that I need Nog . . . That's an order. No, I rescind that. I don't want to push. I'm not overeager. He's coming along nicely. He appeared in the car and on the river. I haven't forgotten his name. My speech and gestures are slower. I don't have to get frantic. I don't need those swift chopping motions with my left hand. I don't pull at my ear as much or look too straight at anyone. I'm coming along. My eyes are wider, my walk looser, my feet more flopping and splayed, my hands rougher, my head angled to the side and slightly downwards, my stomach hollow, my nostrils flared, my hair longer—I have a beard—my breathing more acute, my ass hole tighter. If I could block out the margins I could put it together even more. After all, I'm not sure how I got here, and I didn't bring anything with me, or hardly anything. I can always drop anything excessive over the ledge. I can always manage a story to explain things. Lockett is a small-town con man. That's no trouble. We were visiting a relative in the hospital and felt the need to go south for a vacation. I'm started now. I'll get a fire going and work up an inventory on the cans.

It is night. I built a fire out of creosote wood and counted the cans. There are eighteen cans. I spread the blankets on the ground and placed the knife and canteen within reach. I took off my clothes and placed them near the knife and canteen. It's important to have everything within reach. My jeans and shirt are badly ripped, and the heel of a boot has worn off.

The night is caressing, but my cock has withdrawn further into my stomach. The stars are up there. I can't sleep. The snake is around. I can count on that. Wings brush my head. There are shadows. A black eagle waits above, on the ridge. I know that isn't true. Bats thud against the rocks. The red blinking light from an airplane takes an hour to cross beneath the moon. There is a steady light from the town. But now the light advances up the valley . . . I don't remember when it started, when I couldn't remember any more, when I was cut loose to wander from one place to another. They're closing in. There are more lights now. It started on the beach. I ran into the sea to get away. I had to manufacture memories and a story. My breathing is constricted. Thousands of legs are crawling closer to the fire. I want to keep my body to myself. It was a mistake to remember myself. I can't stop. Nothing has congealed or repeated itself enough to stop. It's the next word that matters. That one word might be a name, the release from a name. Nog. He stands on the other side of the fire, cleaning his harmonica. The sky is black and deep. I have to keep staring into the fire. Lockett and Meridith are inside the area. They crept in while I was distracted. They took advantage of the vacuum. They're inside, whispering. I'm looking at the light from the town. It's better with my back to the fire. They're in the town, sucking and poking each other. I could do with a sleeper, but I would have to crawl too far out of the light. Meridith is Lockett and Lockett is Meridith and they're both inside me, sniffing cocaine. I could suck on an orange. The darkness won't let me make a move. I threw a can into the darkness. "Come in and set," I yelled. Nothing moves, despite the motion out there. They won't cross the circle of light. They're chewing holes in their stomachs. I'm banging on the cans with my knife. I rolled up in the blankets. They're not about to use this log for a sea wall. But it's too hot. I pulled the cans around me and stacked them to make a wall. But one of the cans is still out there. There are only seventeen cans now. I counted them again. Sixteen cans. I must have eaten part of the wall. The fire has to last. In front of me are beans, tuna fish, chicken soup, corned-beef hash, beets, beans, corned-beef hash, beans, chicken soup, spaghetti, tuna fish, hash, corned beef, beans and beets. In that order. Fifteen cans. I miscounted. I have to count over. The hash will be on the bottom of the wall, then the tuna fish, then the beets. The spaghetti and soup will be on the top. The colors dictate it. Let them come now. I'm open. They can move right through me.

It is morning. The sun took care of that. I have stretched. I could sleep now. A bird chirps, otherwise it is quiet. The snake is gone. I went back and dug a hole into the hard earth. I put the bag into the hole and shoved a rock over it. I'm free now to pace out the boundaries of the ledge, stepping briskly from the rear to the edge and then along the sides. It's not a bad walk. I have to find water and poles for a wickiup. I need to say that. It's a relief to have to find water and poles for a wickiup. The cans are neatly stacked and the blankets folded. The Stetson is on top of the packs. I found more creosote wood. The fire lasted until dawn. Now I have to find water and poles for a wickiup. I ripped up my shirt and tied it around my forehead. That works better than the Stetson. If I can find water and poles for a wickiup I might be able to last. My face has puffed up, and there are sores on my legs. I have to throw more away. But not Nog. Nog is all mine. Perhaps when I have rested, when I am not afraid to sleep at night and don't have to keep looking at the town, perhaps then I will walk into town. If I don't like the feel of things I'll continue down the road and over the mountain. There is a jeep parked at the edge of town. A man lies under it. I can see his legs. I want to go for water before it is too late. Nog never worried about water. He could stumble through twenty miles of desert and find water. He doesn't know what it is to hesitate. He would put a stone under his tongue and move on, stepping easily over scorpions and snakes. He's quick-footed, that old boy. He can go a month without talking or remembering anything. A body walked through the town and disappears into an arroyo. A hat is visible, but now it has disappeared. The hat is headed this way. But I have to get my chores done. I have to find water and poles for a wickiup.

I found a trail over the ridge. I slid and scrambled down to a clump of Joshua trees. The trail dropped straight down to where the river cuts through the bottom of a small canyon. I'm down here now. The river is an inch deep where it doesn't stand in stagnant pools. I could stay on here. There is grass, perhaps even fish. I won't have to go for water. There is no ledge to fall over and nothing to be backed up against. The ground doesn't shimmer, and the sky isn't too immense. I can build a house. A shack, anyway. I've got the doctor's bag. That must mean something. I can turn my back, make it on my own. I won't watch the town. Nog makes it on his own. So I claim now this water hole and this canyon and this patch of slimy grass. Lockett is trying to con me. He doesn't want me and Nog to make out. It is something to do with his situation in the town. He wants me to be on the outside, looking in, to give the town a dimension. But I've got myself pointed in another way. I don't have to be useful. I'm tired of being useful to everyone that comes along. I won't move on. That's definite. I'll go back and collect my goods. If I run out I can get supplies from the town. I can trade from what I have in the bag. The nights will be easier here. Mine will be the only light.

I cut three branches from a Joshua tree for the wickiup. I left the poles where I cut them, to pick them up on the way back. I'm on top of the ridge. I can see the ledge below. A girl in jeans and a black flat-brimmed hat sits by the fire. She boils coffee. I'll wait her out. I'll roll over on my back and think of rivers: down the Delaware, the Ohio and the Arkansas. There are whirlpools in the Frazier two hundred feet deep. Logs go around for weeks before they shoot out. Nog knows the Western rivers. Down the Rogue and Humptulips, two thousand miles down the McKenzie. The Eel and the Snake. He wintered by the Columbia. The Sacramento is too tame.

She still squats by the fire. It's too hot. She brings no joyous release, no stirrings within. But she's on my ledge, using my cooking utensils. I took off my clothes. Placing them under my arm, I strolled into camp. "My fire," I said.

She stepped back a few feet. She is very young, her body thin, her eyes startled and blue.

I threw my clothes at her feet. "Sew them," I ordered.

I haven't lost control. Not on my ledge, anyway, not

when I have come back from staking out my own land.

I poured coffee and sat down, my back to her.

"I didn't bring any equipment," she said. Her voice is soft and plaintive. I checked her out from the ridge. She has long dark hair, and her mouth is thin-lipped and open. I lay down on my back. There are rivers I have missed.

"Lockett told me to come," she said. "He said you would cool me out. He said you have traveled through the West, helping people out. I haven't been able to make it. I'm knocked up and I don't know who the father is. But it isn't that. It's supposed to be that way, everyone together and all, no secrets, everyone making it together, contributing and helping out . . . I went through changes when Lockett and Meridith came in. They've taken over. They tell us about you all the time. They build you up plenty. You're supposed to be the one that is keeping us all together, sitting out here and meditating."

At Meridith's name, my cock rose to a thirty-degree angle.

"We're getting into a beautiful organic thing," she went on. "But I keep getting hysterics. I keep flipping and ruining everyone's trip. They put me in a tepee for three days to cool me out, but it didn't work. I've cooked and worked the garden and kept care of the babies and fucked everyone, but I still can't make it. I don't know why."

My cock has become straight as a wickiup pole.

"Do you want me to sit on you?" she asked matter-of-factly. Her eyes, at first filled with tears, have become glazed. She has taken off her clothes.

"I won't object," I said.

She slowly covers me with warm juicy pressure.

Her breasts bob. I started to think of rivers again, but they suddenly came together in one torrential flow.

We lie with our backs on the blanket. The sun sets. The ridge above us becomes red, yellow and then a deep purple. A hawk spirals into a shadow.

"I can't take you with me into this particular night," I said.

She curls next to me and strokes my chest. "I just needed to get out for a while," she said. "While I was on top of you I could see my tepee, and I kept thinking how I would make a new door flap. There are so many things to do. I saw Hank fixing the jeep and Janine picking beans. It looks so peaceful. We have a beautiful thing going for us."

I finally said, "Push that small rock over."

She did as she was told.

"Bring me the bag."

She brought the bag.

"Reach in and let your fingers grab something."

She brought out a vial of pills and a salt shaker. I shook out three pills from the bottle and handed them to her.

"Swallow them," I said.

She swallowed, her eyes moist.

"Keep the salt shaker," I said.

I closed my eyes until she left.

The fire is still alive. A bottle of milk and a paper plate of brown rice lies on the blanket. The fire is too hot and I moved everything back a few feet. I am hungry and I ate.

It is night. I didn't notice. I looked up and the stars had floated out. I'm staring at the fire as if there is nothing else to do. It has died to a few coals. I can't find the strength to build it up. It doesn't protect me from the night, from those feet. They thud in softly now, the toenails huge and flopping, blue with age. There are no voices. There are two lights in the town. . . . I fell out for about five minutes. I have to watch that. But they can come and get me. Let them come, the town, that girl, they can squeeze the breath out of me. I'm off. Off yonder. Off to my valley. I'll build my place, and I won't be facing east or west. They'll never find me. It doesn't matter if it isn't the proper time to build. Nothing happens. Nothing has happened. Nothing is going to happen. I'll learn to love toenails. Nog and I will make out. He can help with the stock. I won't need him inside, by the fire . . . But it's not going to work. I must have been dreaming. The night is too huge, there is too much space, I am shrinking too fast. I must want . . . I lost something, or someone lost something. The space isn't inhabited in the right way. I can't sleep. The noises are within, moving out. If the snake had only been under the rock. I thought of that. I need a corner, a bathtub . . . I name myself master of this ledge. It doesn't help. I have been here before. No, that was Nog. He rushes in now, to be where he is not.

I slept. My arms, as I rocked myself away from the stars, sucked to me like tentacles. I should think about that. Something has become too repeated this far away from the sea. But it is light now and I have to move on. I'm moving on. I've heated coffee. I'm going back through the town and over the mountain. I have my goods lined up. The skillet, coffee pot, cans, knife, can opener and black bag. They're waiting to be packed. Let them wait. One swift sweep of the arm, and I can take care of them all. Either in the pack or over the edge. I've noticed century plants, cholla cactus and cactus wren in the valley. I'll leave the blankets here. Someone might fall by and need a stake. No, I'll take them with me, when I go back down the trail, to my place.

A bullet struck the rocks, the ricochet screaming off to the side. I dropped to the ground.

A horned toad crawls from behind a rock and disappears behind a can of beans. There are rivers I've forgotten. Rivers I've stared at and slept by. Rivers I've bathed in. One river . . . no, that was a road. There have been too many roads.

I made a move for my knife. Nothing happened. I inched towards the edge. I am not able to look over. I am lying on my back, listening to the moan on the ledge below.

The moan rises to a shout and then dies again. I am more relaxed, although the sun is beginning to be unbearably hot.

The moan changed to a curse.

I looked over the edge. I can see a fat shoulder and an arm. The rest is behind a boulder. The boulder is yellow and humped in several places along the top. The arm and shoulder are covered by a khaki shirt. A rifle lies a foot from the clenched fingers. It is not Lockett or Meridith's arm. I am sure of that. It is too fat. I could crawl back and make it over the trail. But he speaks: "Goddamn son-of-a-bitchin-mother-eatin ankle . . . Oooh there, hold it, you ain't damaged that bad. Move for me, old buddy, don't fall out on me, don't swell up like that. Please. Easy now. Easy."

I shoved a can of beans over the edge. Is it true that someone always comes along just in time?

I could go over the big roads. Routes 66, 7, 101, 44, 90 and 22. I could do that. But I prefer dirt roads or small blacktops.

"Listen," a voice pleads. "Listen to me now. I thought you was a sheep. That's God's honest truth. I didn't know forest rangers was around. Never figured anyone to be inspecting or walking around this far out. There's just that town yonder, and if you've seen them you know they're not going to be out here. I thought you was a big horn. I seen something crawling back and forth and I just let fire . . . Listen now . . . my ankle is blued up. It's killing me. Come on over and help me out of here. Don't take it personal. It was just mistaken identity, that's all . . . Say something, will you? Are you up there or are you not up there . . . ? Listen here, I saw a brittlebush on the ridge, and big-horned sheep are always eating brittlebushes. I drove all the way from Tucson for a shot. . . . Are you okay? I didn't hit you, did I? You're not up there dying on me, are you? I can't move . . . ankle hurts real bad. Give me a hand."

I tied the three blankets together and lowered them over the ledge. The body that crawls out from behind the boulder is short and fat. It's covered with a red hunting cap, khaki shirt and pants and polished black boots. The body shrank back.

"Holy mother of God, boy, you ain't got no clothes on."

I pulled the blankets back. I'm sitting near the black bag. I've heated coffee.

"Take it easy, kid," the voice said. "This is an accident. No time for personal feelings. I don't care if you go around like that all the time. I need help, that's all. I'm hurting bad. I was sneaking up for a better position and I had my eyes up on that ledge and I stumbled. I sprained my ankle. Nothing else to it. You got to help me. I wouldn't last a day out here. Course I could fire the rest of my shells, but no one in that town would help me."

I put on my boots, pants and Stetson and lowered the blankets over the ledge. He has his rifle slung over his shoulder. He looks up at me, smiling hopefully. It is an unorganized face with small features lost in the heavy cheeks and fat lips. I braced myself. He managed to climb up.

He lies panting on the ground. "Can't move. Boy I'm played out. Grateful to you. I would have hated to spray that ledge. Them ricochets can hurt a man something terrible."

I brought over the bag and took out some gauze. I picked up the bowie knife.

"Now don't you do it," he said. "I didn't mean nothing. I was joking, is all. No harm in that."

I untied the laces of his boot and slit part of the leather back. His ankle is swollen.

He lies back on the ground.

"I thought you was going to shove that thing into me. You had that kind of look. No disrespect, but I've

seen that look before. Saw it in Iwo Jima and Bataan.
You gave me some kind of one hundred percent fright.
I want to sincerely apologize. Before I move out of
here I'll make it up to you."

I bandaged the ankle.

"Tell you one thing," he said. He wiped his forehead with a red bandanna and takes a long drink from
his canteen. He tries to look at me but can't manage it.
He stares at the glistening stock of his rifle. "Are you
deaf?" he shouted. "Are you deaf or are you deaf and
dumb or don't you want to talk?"

I scratched my name on the ground with the knife.

"Nog. Well, everyone has a right to their own name.
I won't dispute that. Bench is my name. Came in from
Tucson. Got a camper parked near that town. Say
now, you're not the doctor for that town, are you?"

I poured him some coffee.

"I'll get on back to my outfit. It's a Dodge camper
and has all the comforts of home. Now I don't know
who you are, but I'll give you some advice just because
you helped me out. Stay out of that town. It gives me
the creeps every time I get within a hundred yards of
those people. I used to come out here as a boy with my
dad. He would prospect in those old silver mines they
have up on the mountain. It was a ghost town. Still is,
if you ask me. But I used to play in that town all day.
I was sheriff, mayor, bartender and outlaw. Best days
of my life. I owned the whole town. Used to come out
two or three times a year."

He has fallen asleep. He promised only a short nap,
but it has been hours. It is evening. My gear is in
order. I'm set to move out. I could be over the ridge or

down the ledge and he would never know. I could pick up his rifle and pump a bullet into him. I've thought about it. It might be what I need, to hasten a focus. But it's delicate. I don't want to rush things. I don't want to get too dramatic.

He has woken up. He's standing, looking at me suspiciously. He shuffles towards me but he stopped a few feet from me and sat down by the fire.

"We got to build up that fire if it's going to last the night."

I threw creosote wood on the fire. Then I went over to the black bag and took out five pills from a vial. He swallowed them.

It is night. He hasn't said anything. He looks into the fire. At times he seems to be nodding out.

"I loved that town," he said slowly. His words are deliberate and spaced far apart. "My wife, well, we haven't made it in years. My son now, I can't bring him out here. I gave him a .22 and he lost it. Only eleven years old, but when I was seven I had killed rabbits, snakes, frogs, spiders, fish, turtles, cats and a few dogs. I had even managed a shot at a deer. I'm always looking. R. W. Bench is always looking. That's what they say. I'm always looking out for myself. But I got to give that boy something. Just got to. I'm teaching him how to kick. Figure it's the least I can do. I have him out in the backyard every day. He has to kick that ball three hundred times before he gets his supper. My boy will be the number-one football kicker in the Southwest or my name isn't R. W. Bench. That boy is feeble, but he's going to get scholarships and a pro contract. That'll take him up to thirty-five. Then a little business. No, a big business with all those contacts. One million dollars for holding his own ground and sending that ball up higher than the stadium. Those kicks are going to be something to watch. Nobody will believe it. But I'll believe it . . . How long you been sitting here? Who are you, anyway? I don't even recall where I am exactly. I feel so strange. Afraid to sleep. Always have been afraid to sleep. Go to bed every night with four pillows. Done it all my life. My wife, well, she just has to take it, that's all. A man has to be himself. . . . I never seen your likes. I come out for big horn and find you. It don't make sense."

I cooked two cans of beans. We ate. There are seventeen cans.

Bench smokes and looks over the town. There are two lights in the town. His cigarette burns all the way down before it falls from his hand. He lights another. He talks occasionally or mumbles words. I can only make our every third or fourth word: "Back then . . . thirty-seven . . . never rode . . . everything to find . . . tired of coming out . . . no longer, no longer, no longer . . ." I have taken several short walks, back and forth to the ledge and the small cavity and around the fire. Bench sits cross-legged, still talking, his rifle following me. The shadows on the back of the ledge move the rocks closer and then further away. Memories crouch inside me, ready to spring. But they aren't fully formed. I can't recall how I got here, what I went through to get here. Nog watches. He never lets up. He steps forward and then fades away like an Apache. He edges closer. Does he know he is cast loose? That he is abandoned? There is an anger in him, a rage that caused him to smash the furniture in his cabin. That just came to me. His wife cowers in the corner while he puts his fist through the windows. He has never seen her before. His boots are cracked. His shirt torn. He's packed up against the Pacific and has to look back, inside, into the land. He built a corral. He built a goat shed. He planted artichokes. He hustled redwood shakes. He found a forgotten stream and trapped beaver. He made out. But it wasn't good enough. He has to move on. He's sick of the same stands of second-growth Douglas fir. He's tired. He is no longer looking for the octopus. He has forgotten about the octopus.

Bench touches my shoulder. "A third light down there. There hasn't been that much light down there in a hundred years," he says. "I saw the guy who is responsible. I crept up last night. They were in the old saloon. Must have been ten of them. Even a few kids. You never would believe what they had on. All kinds of weird costumes. This one guy was the leader. He was sitting on an overturned washtub, sniffing and drawing in his breath and rolling his eyes up like a nigger. They was passing this long-stemmed pipe around, watching him and looking up to him like he was a coach or manager. He's dressed in these bloomer-type underpants. I'm not kidding. My daddy seen him he would have shot him right there. No questions. They're up to no good. We don't need that kind. Not in that town. I had my sights on him. I had him lined up right through the window. You can't let yourself get pushed around. You got to fight back.

They've taken over the town . . . Boy, you'd better speak up. You're either with me or against me, and this is no time not to know. This is it. This is the last year I'm coming out here and taking that kind of treatment."

He slipped a shell into his rifle.

"You never seen one like this. Built after the old Sharp's buffalo gun. Knock a rabbit's eye out at three hundred yards."

He handed me the rifle.

"Stand guard. Don't let yourself be surprised. I'm tired. I'm so tired. I never been so tired. We got ourselves a day ahead of us. I'll be relieving you in two hours."

He stretched out on a blanket. I'm sitting with my back to the fire. The rifle lies beside me. I could jump over the ledge and disappear or shoot Bench as he sleeps. I've been over that. But it's different now. Plans change. I need to disentangle myself. Although I am inhabiting this place. I'm getting used to it. I'm defending it. I'm watching over someone. That isn't anything to take lightly. And I know this space. I know how precarious it is as related to the whole ridge. I know I can turn around at whatever moment I choose to turn around. The ground has become a rug, the rocks friendly walls. But I'm not listening to myself. Something else is happening . . . If only nothing would grow, nothing change, nothing take hold and join where things take hold and join.

Bench screamed.

"I got bit. The whole place is crawling with spiders."

He waves his arms over his head. Saliva drools from his lips. He tries to stomp on the ground, but his ankle prevents him.

"There was poison making its way across my body," he shouts.

I went over to the bag and took out five yellow and white pills. He swallowed them quickly. He returned to the fire. It is safer by the fire.

Another hour has gone by. Bench tapped me on the shoulder. I handed him the rifle and walked a few times around the fire before lying down on the blanket. I fell asleep.

Bench pounded me on the shoulder.

"Listen, Doc, what they ought to do is fill me with pills. I've been thinking it over. I'm pushing fifty. They could put me way up there for three days and parachute me in to any trouble spot anywhere. Wherever help is needed. I'd wipe out my share before they got me. I'd run into one of their stinking little unwashed hideouts and blast away. That's what they should do with us. It just came to me. Form battalions and drop us in."

He stumbles back to the fire. He is muttering and laughing. I must be on watch again. At least I'm sitting on the edge of the ledge with a rifle in my hands. Bench might have gotten into the bag while I was sleeping. He seems irresponsible. But the dawn is coming. The sun will help out.

Bench crawled up beside me.

"I must have got bit a hundred times. They were coming at me from all sides. I fought them off. We got to get set now. I make it quarter to four. It will be light soon."

His lips have tightened and his pudgy brow is creased into a frown. His eyes protrude before him, unblinking and obsessive.

"You're with me. No time to chicken out. We got to have maximum coordination. This is no dry run. We go in and out fast."

He pointed at the lights from the town.

"I'll work my way down one of the arroyos to the left. That'll bring me up somewhere behind the livery stable. I'll work my way down to the saloon. It should still be dark. My ankle has got to hold. I'll get some tumbleweed and put it on my head. They'll never know the difference. I'll head for the third building down on the left from the mountain. That big light comes from there. They're all in there. You sneak down one of the arroyos to the right. Come in low on the other side. Give me a distraction. Pound on something. I'll do the rest. You got your knife? Oh, Jesus, he don't have his knife."

He limped back to the fire. He's looking for the knife. I need to move on anyhow. I might as well make it today. I might walk through the town and over the mountain. Either that or strike out over the desert. I can follow the road. That's enough of a plan. I have water. I'm in excellent shape. I've developed a suntan. My hair is bleached from the sun. I don't smoke.

Bench came back with the knife. His pupils have enlarged. He grins slyly, holding the knife in the palm of his hand, balancing it in a throwing position.

"As a doc, you might have your own idea how

things have to be done. But I know about the wilderness. I know what it took to discover and hold this country . . . Course you might not be a doc. I know you can hear. Known that for a long time. You heard me when I was lying down on the ledge. Otherwise how come you came over and lowered the blankets? . . . I'm not going to report you. Relax. I know you're not helping them. I figure they moved you out when they moved in. You were probably working in one of the mines, prospecting a little and living in the town. The bastards turned you out. You weren't harming anyone. Just a crazy desert rat. Right? They got to know someone else is out here too. You know what I'm talking about? Of course you know what I'm talking about. You wouldn't be nodding at me if you didn't. I know that. I've been coming out here all my life. I've got a Dodge camper. No one owns up to what he has more than me. A man's got to have claims. If he doesn't defend his claims he's hardly a man."

He threw the knife into the ground, a few inches from my foot.

"Pick it up. Pick up the knife if you're with me . . . Course I don't need you. I can do it alone. If you ain't with me, move ass out of here. Go on, get out. I've had my eyes on this ledge before you was born. Fact is, I'm claiming this ledge as my own."

I picked up the knife.

"You're in it now. I knew you had it in you. You're not about to be pushed around same as the next man."

He dropped to his knees, crouching forward on the balls of his feet. "This piece of country and that town is ours. You'd better believe it. Hut hut hut. When the ball is snapped we got to move. Hut hut."

He swayed and fell. His face hit the ground a few inches from my left foot. He sat back. Then he groaned and rolled to one side and looked up.

"We got ourselves a contract," he said. "We're in the whole thing together. We're brothers. No turning back. When it's over I'll escort you out of this stadium and buy you a steak dinner at the first diner. We got ourselves an agreement, and we didn't have to sign no papers or draw no blood."

We broke camp. I left the cans a few feet from the rear of the ledge. I piled them up neatly, in a line. There are sixteen cans. I dropped a can of tuna fish into the black bag. I folded the blankets and left them behind the cans. I want to have something to recognize if I come back. I won't be back. But I want to know I can come back if I find myself coming back. I don't want any surprises. Perhaps, if I recognize the cans, I'll be able to find the rest of the trail, over the ridge and down to the river.

I have my canteen and a pack. I'm wearing what is left of my boots, my pants and a Stetson. I don't remember what happened to my shirt. I haven't found anything to put into the pack. I took it off and left it in back of the cans. I have the black bag. I no longer think of the black bag as a doctor's bag. I haven't looked inside it yet. Not that I can remember. I put the knife in the bag. The bag isn't any heavier. The handle still grips. The black surface is still intact except for two patches on one side where it is worn and scuffed. It feels familiar when I approach it and stoop to pick it up. It carries closer to the body and doesn't annoy my thigh even on the most difficult climb or descent. It is still dark. I've tried not to notice the stars. I have managed to forget the moon. It has been too big, too present to mention. But the stars reflect themselves everywhere. There is no place to hide from the stars. There are too many. I've spent most of my time in an endless search to find light and get away from light. If I could only be sure of that, that nothing happened. It would summon something, a continuity perhaps, a shout anyway; no, I don't have the energy to get carried away. I am being carried away. I need something steadier, an endless stare. The wall of rock is flat. Nog is closer, his eyes cruel and distant.

Bench whistled. He agreed to whistle, back on the ledge, as a signal. He has a flat toneless two-note whistle. His whistles grow faint. They have stopped. We found a way down the lower ledge—Bench knew the way all along—and then slid down a steep decline to the edge of the valley. It must be a valley. It lies between two high points. The one directly in back and the one somewhere in front. But beneath the surface, in the web of canyons and arroyos, it no longer feels like a valley. We huddled together. Bench put his hand on top of mine and I put my other hand on top of his and he put his other hand on top of mine. Our embrace fell apart when he threw up his right hand in a stiff salute. Carrying his rifle at high port, he stumbled off into a huge canyon. I chose a smaller opening, an arroyo. I am working my way parallel to him. In any case, I have gone another way.

descended. I am involved in an uncontrolled stumble. I fell. It is difficult to enter narrow passages with steep walls on either side. It is darker. The darkness is oppressive, as if it has been trapped here for centuries. I have delayed the dawn. I have returned into the center of the night. The ground is uneven and rough. Prickly bushes thicken my forward movement. I am afraid of snakes. I am afraid. This route is obviously rarely traveled. I am unable to feel my way. The walls press in, and the more I touch and fall against the walls, the more the walls press in. I am groping. At least my ragged feet are groping. My hands are push-

ing out in front of me. They're no help. I can't smell,
lick or see anything. The walls are twenty to a hundred
feet apart. I discovered that by banging from one wall
to another. Each bump shrinks the distance. The walls
are closer together now. The sky is up there. I counted
thirty-seven stars. They don't give off heat. They don't
show the way. Boulders are bulbous noses. I sat down
on one. I want to reach into the bag, but my hand
won't reach. It is the bag, not what is inside it. The air
is dry, as if at any moment it might ignite. I have to
move on. I said that. I need to remind myself. If I
forget for a moment I'm lost . . . It is happening, it has
happened, it might continue to happen . . . A tread
moves into position directly in back of me. It stops and
I'm going on. I'm not going back. If I turned around I
would still be going forward. Best to press on. If I only
had a flashlight to check out the fossils. The whole
area must be crawling with fossils. If I could go from
fossil to fossil I wouldn't tremble in front of every
hole, every overhang, every crevice, every nose.
Breathing forms wait for a hesitant step. I peed
against a giant nose. I tried to throw up, but there isn't
anything inside. I'm hungry. There is the can of tuna
fish in the bag. But I left the can opener on the ledge.
I'm not developed enough to pry it open with my
teeth. I took a sip from the canteen. There is only half
a finger of water left. I yelled. My voice didn't come
back. Something must have happened between the
giving out and the coming back. I yelled again, and a
voice came back. It isn't my voice. My voice is in back
and in front of me and along the sides. My voice is
trapped in a huge hallway. But it's silent now. I think

it's silent. No, it's still dribbling out. The hallway has no doors leading off it, no relief, no stairway or another wall at the end. The hallway or the cunt, the alley, even the arroyo, anything will do, just to be sure, to know that it twists and bends, curves and cuts into an angle, that it leads somewhere. I might have doubled back on myself. I might be caught in a vicious circle. I have to try and not remember where I'm going, what I'm in, exactly, in order to have the courage to get there . . . There is nothing more to invent, nothing more to play with . . . I know Nog is caught, I have known it for some time, that he is paralyzed with his foot in the stirrup, one leg half over the horse's ass. I know he's reached the end of the woods, that the light has gone out of his chest, that he's changed his clothes, that his speech is clipped and brutal. There is no relief there, to know he is moving back, towards the city. I am in an arroyo. I had forgotten. I don't need the dark, the wet, the suck. I cried and shrank back because this might not be an arroyo. Who told me it was an arroyo? Was it Bench? He was confusing me by inventing the terrain, making it safe, to get my food, he might have gone back and stolen my cans. He has my bandages. How long have I been going through this passage, and who was it that made me think it was a passage? It has always been like this, the endless passageways, the detours, the stops, the same whimpering complaints. I have bored myself enough to have gone on without noticing I am going on. I whistled. A toneless two-note. I'm climbing now and whistling at the same time. The ground is sandier, and the walls are crumbling. The walls have disintegrated.

I am in back of a tepee. The light is at the other end of town. I crouched. But no one is about. It is still dark. We miscalculated back on the ledge. The stars are no help. The stars are never any help. A slight wind wheezes off the desert. I crept on all fours to the closed flap of a tepee, the bag between my teeth. I dropped the bag and put my cheek against the skin of the tepee. It is taut and cool. I listened for Bench's whistle, but I can hear nothing. I stood up and looked back, shielding my eyes as if there is something to shield my eyes from. There is a small point of light. It might be the dying fire on the ledge or perhaps another star. I crawled through the flap. Coals glow softly in the middle of the round space. I inhaled incense and stale sweat. There are three or possibly four bodies lying on blankets around the coals. The bodies are entwined, making it difficult to distinguish where one begins and the other leaves off. I crawled around the inside of the tepee, completing two full circles. I want to wrap an arm or a leg around another limb and breathe deeply. But there is a pressure inside me, enough to keep me from a prone position. I'm probably not tired. The three or four bodies are two children, asleep in each other's arms. I crawled towards a crate on the outer edge of the circle, directly across from the flap. I picked up a rusty Ballantine Ale can filled with colored glass beads. I threw the beads on the ground, as if they were dice. I made three small circles, one within the other. I discovered two water-color brushes on the crate, plus a diaphragm, a safety razor, a small ivory duck's head, four toothbrushes, a pocketbook, a box of crayons, two full-length blue pencils, a rubber doll's head, a large bottle of Anacins and a rubber PT boat. I took the doll's head and the pocketbook and crawled out of the tepee. I dropped them into the bag and crawled back, placing a button and three tongue depressors on the crate. A body stirs and mumbles in sleep.

"Daddy says two . . . fired her leg . . . yellow bush . . ."

I crawled out of the tepee. No one is about. I picked up the bag and walked around the tepee. There are three tepees, and the town lies below. Lights shine at the far end of town. I walked to the street. It is lighter. Gouged gullies run across the street. There are a dozen buildings on each side. It's never easy to stroll into a strange town. I took eight steps forward. My feet stopped. Weeds have filled in the spaces where the boardwalk has fallen through. A hitch rail has fallen over. Broken glass lies scattered in front of empty windows. I can make out a few signs: ENO'S ROOM AND BOARD . . . GENERAL MERCHANDISE . . . BLACKSMITH SHOP . . . ASSAY OFFICE. There is a jail and a hotel. I heard a series of bell-like tinkles and then silence. I grasped the handle of the black bag as if it was the handle of a Colt .45. I took four more steps. Nothing happened. Nothing ever happens when I take four more steps. I took five fast steps and stopped. I can hear voices or the drone of one voice, towards the light at the end of the street. The light comes from a bright blue building. I noticed the color thirty steps ago, but it didn't register. Nothing registers at the beginning of a street. I have to invent it all. I darted to one side. I don't want to be suddenly aware of someone walking slowly towards me, facing me in the middle of the street, coming on. Nor do I want to be caught in a cross fire. The boards creak and the sturdy weeds brush my body. The weeds are over six feet, with white flowers at their tops. Moving forward, Nog shrinks back, into a damp basement. Is he looking for memories? Does he need that kind of support . . . ? I passed an empty bunkhouse. I bent over in the familiar crouch and sprinted to the side of the blue building. A white sign with a yellow cactus in the center hangs over the front door. The blue paint on the side of the building is wet. Light streams through a cracked stained-glass window. The panes are dark red and blue, with a plastic cactus imposed over a black cross. On the bottom of the frame I can read in large gothic letters:

Anna Wigglesworth Class of 1968.

I sank to the ground, my back to the building. The paint sticks to my back, making me an extension of the wall. It is lighter. I am tired. I was moving too fast down the street. I should have slept in the tepee. But I was moving towards something; I thought there was a place to move towards. I've come to a place. I should leave before it becomes a place I was going towards. It doesn't matter. I can't move. In front of me garbage spills over the sides of a large cardboard box. There is a pile of broken furniture. A bell tinkles. Someone giggles. I can hear a voice or two voices inside the building: ". . . the way it is. Lines. You can't depend on lines. I put green down one side. Left this side alone. Ocher is . . . Hmmm . . . Ocher is nice. Pull that around here. This side is taken care of, if you see what I mean. . . . Okay . . . Hung just thinking on . . . the one side."

"Spread it out . . . Give me . . . Just a little. Down on my knees, spreading it out. I have my ten-by-ten smooth. . . . Hmmm . . . Not forever . . . That was good. No pebbles. Not one bump in that ten-by-ten. One twig, and I do something, anything, go back to town, try the lookout, take something. Then I sprint back to the ten-by-ten and get that twig and break it up and chew it and swallow it . . . Working the land, you understand . . . Stalks coming up so fine. Rhythm is the secret . . . It's not arithmetic. Those two plastic hoses come down from opposite sides of the reservoir. I put down lime this evening, a shake across the top, nothing much, then sandy loam . . . so fine . . . Changing my name to Sandy Loam . . . Seven stalks already over six feet. No transplanting. They're all arranged three and a half feet from each other. Chicken wire stretched tight to keep varmints out . . . Everyone's got breathing room in my area. We'll make the bread."

"What's he doing now?"

"Sitting in front of the cactus."

"Break your neck to turn around."

"He's holding it."

"Been on a long time."

"In and out."

"Two sniffs are enough to keep this crowd together."

I must have fallen asleep. It is lighter. It is almost morning. I must have dozed. That's good enough. I dozed. I bent forward, as if trying to touch the ground. The paint sticks to my back. I stood up. Falling forward removed me from the voices. Either that or the voices stopped. I picked up the bag and moved to the next window. I pressed my face towards the light. My face fell forward, there being no pane in the window. My head is inside the room.

There is no mirror behind the bar except for three jagged pieces. The pieces have been painted black, perhaps to extinguish any reflection. Two shelves hold shot glasses and empty bottles. The walls are covered with a heavy layer of dust. Cobwebs surround two fans hanging from the ceiling and a broken chandelier. Colored beads hang from nails on the wall. There are no chairs and tables. Five mattresses are grouped together in the center of the room. Candles stuck in the floor cast dim beacons of light. The mattresses are occupied, although limbs and one head drag on the floor. Three men in black robes and long beards sit on one mattress. Everyone else sleeps or appears to be either falling into or out of sleep. One of the men strikes a triangle with a spoon. One pats a palm slowly over a narrow drum. The last plays with a pile of broken glass. Lockett sits on a washtub at the end of the room. The washtub is covered with a black and white Navaho rug. Behind him stands a huge saguaro cactus extending through a hole in the ceiling. Six arms, like tentacles, break off at right angles from the stem, and point upwards. Lockett might be asleep, although his lips suck in and out. A niche in the center of the cactus holds a small candle. The light from the candle, like a glowing eye, falls softly over

Lockett's hair and white empire gown. The folds of the gown have been arranged so that his limbs are invisible.

A hand presses my back.

"You have a white hand on your back."

The voice sounds like Meridith's.

"And I have a blue hand."

I can feel her sitting down. I moved a leg against her back to be sure. A rifle barrel has appeared in the window directly across from me. Except for the drummer, the trio on the mattress has dozed off. No one else moves. It is easier not to notice anyone else moving. The rifle circles the room and stops at Lockett.

"I heard you were about," Meridith said.

She has pressed her head against my thigh.

"Lockett said you would come. He figured you would be down to your last three cans."

The rifle has disappeared.

I can't be seen. Or my head can't be seen. My back is visible. It must have been visible to Meridith. It is Meridith, after all. How long has she been watching me? Did she follow me from the tepee?

I heard a soft whistle.

Meridith lifts my foot and takes off my shoe. She places my foot in her lap. It feels as if she is wearing rough jeans. She rubs my foot.

"You've been walking for such a long time. You smell terrible. You can't be seen with the bag. Too much has been said. Too many strung-out people are waiting to get at the bag."

She tries to take the bag. I shifted it to the other hand.

"You're too early," she said. "More people were supposed to make it with you on the ledge. It's delicate here. You can't come barging in. We haven't got all the donations we had hoped for. Not enough has happened. Lockett has more cans for you. We'll put some cans in the bag and take out some of the other stuff. You can sneak back right away."

The rifle has reappeared in the window.

"It takes time, darling." She still rubs my foot. "You can stand a few more days out there. We've been working too, you know. We haven't been goofing. We built a stone reservoir and planted a crop."

I can hear whispering again, but I can't hear the words. There must be two figures under the stained-glass window. Meridith pulls on my leg.

"You can at least look at me. My hair is longer. You could let yourself say something. How do you know who's rubbing your foot? I'm known as Girl-Who-Is-Not-Afraid-of-Six-Red-Horses . . . I wish that were true. Oh, Nog, make some kind of a move."

She strokes my ankle. Two figures rise from a mattress and walk slowly towards the door. Nog has disappeared. I said that before. But I need a memory. I need two memories. With two working for me, I might be able to make a move, even if it's back, towards the ledge. I can always fake going back. But I've forgotten what is needed, what it will take to push me forward.

The rifle fired.

Lockett's arms spread straight out from the gown. They stiffen and reach towards the ceiling before clutching at the hole in his stomach. There are three holes, from the ceiling to the niche in the cactus to the hole in his stomach. All neatly lined up. Lockett moans and falls back, into the cactus. Thorns rip into his gown and pinion him to the cactus. His head jerks forward, but he doesn't fall. The candle toppled to the floor. Most of the forms on the mattresses have awakened.

Meridith screams and claws my leg. A man rushes towards Lockett and beats at the gown, which has started to smolder. I swung the bag at Meridith's head, knocking her to the ground. I ran towards the bunkhouse, stooping once to put on my boot. The bunkhouse turned out to be the bunkhouse, although there are no bunks. I can watch the street through a window. Men run towards the saloon. A small boy cries near the side of a building across the street. A woman grabs him and disappears with two men into the arroyo at the end of the street. Others run the opposite way. A jeep careens wildly down the street. Someone has run into the bunkhouse and is yelling at me. I climbed out the window. As I ran into the next building another shot went off. I am in the lobby of a hotel. The stairway is boarded up. The windows are broken. I smelled smoke and ran into the building across the street. It is the office of the *Sentinel*. Yellowed newspapers lie on the floor. The machinery is old, and print lies everywhere. Meridith looks in the window. I sat down. I can't see her. But I must be waiting for her. She has dropped beside me. "Nog is shot," she said.

"Lockett was shot."

My voice won't come out. I haven't spoken in so long. I tried to push words out, but nothing happened.

"Don't cry," Meridith said. "It was Lockett. He was calling himself Nog for a while. I get confused. It was Lockett."

Another shot rang out. Glass shattered.

"We have to get shut of here," Meridith said matter-of-factly. She is crying.

"It was Bench," I said.

"You said Lockett."

"Bench did in Lockett."

Meridith tilted up her face and bit my neck. I tasted the tears on her cheek. "You're overwrought," she said. She licks my cheek. "He might not be dead. If he's dead it's all over. It's all over anyway. He didn't have long to go. I can't think about it. I can't think. Fuck me."

I bent her over a table, her back pressing into type face. The paper on the floor, beneath her hanging head, describes a gold strike in Tuscarora, Nevada, in 1870. Nog has passed quietly through Nevada. He's not wasting time. He has lost weight. He has raped two college girls in Colorado and Arkansas.

My pants had fallen to my ankles when the door opened. "In here," a voice yelled. "He's raping her."

A bullet slammed into the wall. The man ran away.

"Come and get it, boy." It is Bench from across the street. I have my head out the window. He's waving at me. "Almost shot you a second time. Only got two bullets left. I messed em up good. Meet you south, at the Dodge. Follow the road. I got to get me two more."

He disappeared behind the hotel. A man in a black robe ran into the doorway. He has a bow and arrow.

He is either aiming at me or Meridith. A bullet shot the heel off his right boot. I heard Bench shout and then scream. The man in the doorway has fallen forward. I pulled up my pants.

Meridith and I climbed out the back window. She took my hand and led me into a shallow wash. We crept past the town and found the road up the mountain. We went past the tepees, one of which is burning, and stopped in front of a cave or mining excavation. Meridith disappeared into the black opening.

I don't need any kind of a cave, even the beginnings of a cave. That's over. I can see the town beneath us. One more shout rang out. That was an hour ago. Meridith must be resting, or perhaps she has gone through the cave to emerge at the other side of the mountain. The sun is climbing to its highest point. Two houses burn. I can see the web of arroyos and the ledge halfway up the ridge. I don't want to look. I put my fist in front of my face, but the margins are too big. I can still see an arroyo and smoke from the town. It is hot. Perhaps Meridith has trapped me into being a lookout while she disappears. But I can hear her moving around. I need help from Nog. I can admit that now. But he doesn't notice. He's crossing a muddy river on a flat-bottomed boat. A crowd of people grimly watch him cross to the other side.

Meridith appeared in time to see Bench staggering from the door of the saloon. He lands sagging on his knees in the middle of the street. We are moving on. Meridith holds my right hand. My left is curled over the handle of the bag.

We followed the road over the mountain. The road

crossed the mountain and then dropped to the desert. We found the Dodge camper. The key is in the ignition. Meridith got in the driver's seat. I lay down on the bunk and fell asleep as Meridith started the engine and drove away.

don't want to look around. The bunk is comfortable.
I know I'm going to look around. Meridith is driving, and the radio plays Western music. We're traveling very fast. We might be following someone or being
followed. I've been asleep. Either that or I've had my
eyes closed. There is a small icebox in one corner and
a clothes rack in the other, full of swaying slacks and
jackets; a cardboard box with five bottles of gin and a
gun rack holding three rifles and a shotgun. I made a
list on the wall. I must have scrawled it out with grease
from the gun rack. My fingers are black. I have my
eyes open, reading the list. Nog interrupts. He

crouches in the corner of a boxcar, holding a switchblade knife in front of him. Two men in Bermuda shorts and soft gray fedora hats warily circle him, blackjacks hanging loosely from their fingers. He's forgotten where he's going, where he's come from. I must have dreamt that or am still dreaming. It's easier as a dream, more lucid, even if it isn't a dream. The trees gave out on him. He couldn't sit and whittle among a stunted second growth. I must have said that. I need to recite something over and over. The list on the wall is not enough. I have to add to the list, keep on adding, never stop adding to the list. The camper is air-conditioned. Lockett is air-conditioned. Someone did him in. I think I remember that. Either that or no one did him in. It might have been a performance. I don't want to know. We're rolling on. I must have said that. But we're rolling on, and that is a recognition.

Meridith pulled over to the side of the road. She slid out of the front seat and opened the rear door. She looks in on me, her hands on her hips. Her hair is pulled loosely behind her by a rubber band. She has put on pale lipstick and heavy eye shadow. She is thin, thinner than I remember, even in her oversized and torn blue jeans and soiled tee shirt. She pulled the blanket I am lying on out from under me. She is gone. The light from the open door is blinding. I'm not about to go outside. I've been outside. Meridith crawled inside. She opens the icebox and takes out bread, cheese, tomatoes and sliced ham. She has crawled outside. She returns for a bottle of gin and crawls out again. There is room to stand. That's no problem. I stood up and added islands to the list: Mallorca,

Crete, Lesbos, Long Island, Curaçao, Haiti, Cuba, Madagascar, Ceylon, Wolfe Island, the Azores, Tahiti and Governors Island. It doesn't help. I crawled outside. Then I crawled inside. The light is too intense, the sky too huge. There is too much space. Nothing moves. It is too silent. We're parked on a plateau surrounded by sandstone buttes. It's like an ancient abandoned city. The rock has been eroded and shaped by the wind. I don't need monuments. There is sage and patches of lichen. I'm staying inside.

I crawled outside.

Meridith has spread the blanket on the sand. She is eating a sandwich. I walked slowly to the blanket, my eyes focused on the sand in front of me. I can't manage the sky or the buttes. I walked around the blanket. It's a yellow blanket. Meridith prepares another sandwich. The last sandwich I ate was at Smitty's, a quarter of a mile down the beach. I can't remember beaches. I'm not sure I've ever been on a beach. But I suppose it was on a beach where I first began to ruminate. I was recovering from something. I forget the ailment. But I was breathing in and out, just trying to get through the days. Then I collapsed and tried to begin again. That must be it.

I sat down.

"We're sitting on billions of shells," I said. I want to check out the sound of my voice. "This whole plateau is crammed with bones. We're shells ourselves."

Meridith lies on her back. She chews loudly. I could make a move and grab the blanket out from under her, but I keep walking around it. I don't want to collapse. I don't want to look too suddenly at the sky. To protect myself, I walk around the blanket.

Meridith finished her sandwich. She speaks while looking at the sky. "If you think we're staying here, you're wrong. This place spooks me."

The girl sat up and took a long pull from the bottle of gin.

I don't remember seeing this particular girl. Of course, she must be Meridith. At one point in the last few days she said she was Meridith. She made a point of saying that. But when exactly was that? She certainly looks like Meridith. I'll stand on that. But something has changed. Something must have slipped in or out somewhere along the line. Perhaps it's her voice.

She looks up at me. "You killed Lockett. You wanted to be Lockett, and when he abandoned you on the ledge you had him killed."

I am walking faster around the blanket. It's too hot to break into a trot, although I feel like punishing myself. Why isn't Nog walking out from the deep shadow of a monument, striding steadily towards us?

"You finessed the whole operation beautifully." She took another pull from the bottle. "Leading me on. Jumping on my bones whenever I had my back turned. Dipping into the bag. You've been evil with that bag."

She is sobbing. Her voice is suddenly tiny and petulant.

"You don't understand. You've never understood."

My steps have slowed. It is very hot. I'm perspiring. I can't keep on. I have to keep on. Where is Nog, now that I need him? Surely I have said that. Surely there is no need to count on that any more. But he might sneak back before it is too late. He might have received the signal. I should crawl back to the camper. I need the anonymous hum of the air conditioner. On the way out of the camper I noticed a few objects to add to the bag. That is something to look forward to. A canteen. A photograph of a football team. A watch band. A key chain . . . The canteen might not fit. I can add that to the list on the wall . . . The horizon is breaking up. I check it out briefly when I reach an edge of the blanket. I travel exactly around the square, wearing a rut in the sand, pivoting sharply when I come to a left or right face. There are four diaphanous platforms hanging in the sky. They have changed from vermilion to deep purple. The monuments seem to be receding. Two of them have crumbled to dust. Meridith sits quietly. I might risk a swift move for the sandwich beside her knee. She stares through the bottle, perhaps at the blanket, perhaps at a small lizard crawling across the blanket.

She looked up. Her face is flushed and radiant.

"You've been dipping into the bag. You profane son of a bitch."

I'm walking in two-four time. I want to stretch out on the blanket. Despite the heat, I want to lie down on the blanket and eat a sandwich. I don't mind not being in the camper. But I can't keep on. I'm in the best shape of my life, but I might not be able to keep on.

"I lost the sound of my beautiful voice," Meridith said. Her voice has become hard and nasal. "For over a year other voices kept getting in the way. Now I'm getting it back again. When you did away with Lockett it did wonders for me. I've been lying here, realizing it I'm getting my voice back again. Lockett wasn't my type, you know. I was mad for him and I'll continue what he set out to do, but it was hard. It's difficult being around a man with vision. It's different with you, of course."

I sat down and grabbed the sandwich. I finished it in three bites. I lay back and closed my eyes. But I opened them right away. Meridith is sprinting towards the camper. I ran after her. I must have run with my head down because when I got to the front seat she wasn't there. She must be in the back. I crawled in.

She points a rifle at my head. Her eyes are wide and blank. She smiled mysteriously as she pulled the trigger. The gun isn't loaded. She put the rifle back in the case.

"You can help with the driving," she said.

She lay down on the bunk. I sit at her feet. I raised her foot and kissed the instep. She closed her eyes.

"You can have me if you want to," she said.

There is too much to remember. I need three memories now.

"You want to shoot up?" she asked.

"No."

"You're afraid of anything too overt," she said sweetly. "I know all your little boyish secrets. I might as well tell you a little about what is happening, now that you seem to be along. We have fifteen hours of driving ahead of us. We'll pop dexies and make it straight through. Lockett booked passage for two on the first of the month. We have to make one quick stop, but we'll get there in time. Lockett didn't know that I knew.

When you shot him I went up to the cave to get the tickets. He hid everything there. Five hundred dollars as well as a few notes."

I put down her foot. I thought she was asleep, but on a closer look I noticed her eyes were half open. "Might as well get on with it," she said. "I'll get ice for the gin. You bring the clothes."

I followed her, my arms full of clothes from the rack.

I dropped the clothes in the middle of the blanket.

She handed me a glass of gin.

We raised our glasses. The sky and the horizon have settled down. There is only the heat. I can handle the heat. Something happened in the camper. Something about a plan, about not being able to be part of a plan. I don't trust plans. Meridith rummages through the clothes. We could hunt each other around the buttes. That might be a way to work it out. The survivor can drive away in the camper. But I am helpless before a plan. She must know that. I could hang her scalp in my belt. Or she could hang my scalp in her belt. But that has all been done before. I am so tired. I might as well embrace the plan. I will anyway.

She threw me a Spanish-style jacket of buckskin, fringed in the Indian manner. I put it on. She took off her tee shirt and replaced it with a long-sleeved khaki shirt. It is too big for her, but she rolled up the sleeves and tucked the ends into her jeans. She looks cleaner and more efficient.

She went back to the camper. I lay down on the blanket and leaned my head against the pile of clothes. I shut my eyes. I'm not about to make any sudden movements. She can trust me on that score. The jacket is too big, but I enjoy the looseness. The sun is unbearable. The sun must always be unbearable when the victim is stretched out on the sand.

Meridith's mouth presses into mine. Her tongue parts my clenched teeth and arrives roundly at my own tongue. I opened my eyes.

She kneels over me, the black bag by her side.

She sits back on her heels, reaching into the bag. Her eyes never leave mine. She brings out a button, a torn piece of cloth and a syringe. She places them on the blanket and dips her hand in again. She produced two plastic vials and a matchbox.

"Someone switched the dexies into a matchbox," she complained. "We ain't got many matches and we got so far to go." She dropped two dexies with a gulp of gin.

"We have to get rid of the camper," she said. "We have to arrive with nothing but a full bag. We have to sell it."

"We could cover a lot of ground with that camper," I said. "Build an octopus, put it on a truck bed and hustle the West. We could see rivers, mountains, beaches, trees, hamlets, towns, cities and even a few islands."

She doesn't answer. She might not have heard. She looks preoccupied. I put everything that had been taken out of the bag into the bag, plus the cap from the empty gin bottle. We are moving on. We have been moving on.

Meridith took some notes out of her pocket and put them in the bag. I gathered the clothes together and tied the blanket around them. I slung the blanket over my shoulder and threw it in the back of the camper. Meridith handed in the bag.

"I'll take the first shift," she said.

I'm sitting on the bunk with the bag between my legs. We are driving very fast. There is something pressing, something I have to do. But I forget. Nog and I are splitting the country between us, straining at opposite ends. He has crossed Ohio. I am heading the other way. I found a case of shells in the bottom of the gun rack. I dropped it into the bag. I have to lie down. I'm lying down, cushioned against bumping from one place to another. Powder River, the Musselshell, Ambush Creek. That's better. The other list is already dated. I've never been on those rivers. Nog hated the octopus. That becomes clear. He couldn't admit they were shy and intelligent. He wanted a giant squid with fifty-foot arms, enough to pull down a redwood. He was reaching out too far. He wanted a reputation. His own arms have almost been chopped off. At the very least, they're bleeding. A vein has been sliced open. One arm is in a sling. He won't settle for a long drive and a soft sucking body at the end. Octopi see better than most men. They don't miss a move, even in the darkest of caves. I can't face this. I wish I could encircle a breast. If I could only forget she is driving, that we are moving so fast, so deliberately. If only the octopus were trailing behind us on a truck bed. Perhaps it is. I can manage that. My cock has become stiff. A moray eel can destroy an octopus in three seconds. I could put a shell into a rifle, but I've put enough shells into the bag. I'm partial to shells. I don't need to think about sperm whales. I need to be rubbed down and put out. My breathing is labored. She was vulnerable lying on the green blanket in the sand, on top of billions of shells.

I put the bag into the icebox. I found another case of shells in the bottom of the gun rack. I loaded the double-barreled shotgun and rolled down the rear window. We're traveling through flat empty land. The narrow blacktop falls straight back until it disappears into a slight haze. I can see for miles on all sides. There is no car in sight. I waved the gun back and forth, covering the whole landscape. You can pick up a few tricks if you watch people and objects closely enough. A vulture rose slowly from a dead rabbit. I pulled the trigger. I missed the vulture but hit the rabbit. I must have been aiming for the rabbit. I squeezed the other trigger to hear the sound again, to empty both barrels. I reloaded. Meridith hasn't slowed down. In fact, she has speeded up. She must be doing eighty miles an hour. I took a bottle of gin from the cardboard box and drank from the bottle with one hand. With the other hand I blasted a vulture. He dropped onto the middle of the road. I love the smell of cordite. It would be satisfying to skin these wild beasts. But there is no time. We are involved in a plan. We have to be somewhere at some particular time. At least I understood it that way. I have to keep up a steady line of fire the way they managed to drop buffalo and Indians from train windows. The camper has filled with acrid smoke. Meridith has turned up the radio. It's a symphony. She weaves the camper back and forth across the road, slowing down now whenever there's a target. I missed a road runner but split a rattlesnake in two. I've loaded a .30–30. Anything that moves receives a barrage. I blasted a Coke bottle. I prefer the shotgun, but the .30–30 has a decent feel. It's a steady piece. I bagged an octillo cactus with it. I left a rabbit spread out on the steaming blacktop. Meridith has run over a few rabbits herself. Another car is visible, coming on slowly. A fence appeared without warning. I let go with both barrels of the shotgun. The car is coming on. There are cattle now on both sides of the road. I threw the empty gin bottle out, but it smashed on the road before I could get a shot at it. The cattle look stringy and mean. We must be approaching grasslands. I dropped a black cow to her knees with the .30–30. I got another one with a shot through the neck. I bagged two cows standing together with both barrels of the shotgun. I'm improving. If I had a .45 I might be more efficient. At least I could pick up more of the small stuff. As it is I'm cleaning up the road nicely. The car is visible now. It's a black convertible. There are two people in the front seat. There should be an aquarium in here, on top of the icebox, to balance the view outside. My eyes are burning. But they're steady. I could drill a hawk at two hundred yards. I wish there was a horse galloping alongside. I could do with a good stallion. I'm moving the .30–30 back and forth. I want to take my time. I want to make this clean. I took off my Stetson and wiped my forehead. I've got a good list going for me. I don't want to spoil it: rabbits, snakes, vultures, fence posts, Coke bottles, Esso oil cans, cows, one bull and a road runner. Meridith has slowed down. She's driving steadily. We're in perfect harmony. We're coordinated. She anticipates my slightest wish. A man and a woman in the car. Three hundred yards. Two hundred yards. The man is driving. My breathing is still regular and controlled. I know what to do. I don't have to think. But the car has dropped back. I wiped off the guns with a dishrag and put them back in the case. We pick up speed, I kneeled on the bunk and reached into the front seat to encircle Meridith's right breast with my right hand. It is a smaller breast than I have imagined. But it is round and firm. I don't remember having touched it before.

I lay back on the bunk and fell asleep.

We've turned off the road. The bumps woke me. We must be on a dirt road. I don't want to look. It's evening. I got through the day. It went fast enough. A nap helps. Meridith has turned the radio off and is driving very slowly over the dirt road. The dexies must have had no effect if I slept so well. Perhaps I forgot to take them. I didn't dream. I would like to lie here, with my arms behind my head. I would like to lie here for a few days. We have stopped.

Meridith opened the front door. I can hear her voice but I can't distinguish the words. Another voice is louder. It is low and hoarse and I can make out several of the words:

"Long time. No use askin . . . rough times. Since '43 . . . '52 pickup. Chevy. Got to look through it . . . come far . . . up in the Mogollons."

They must have walked away. A dog barks. I should sit up and think about stepping outside. There might be a transaction going on. But I'm still lying on the bunk. My hands are still behind my head. I have my eyes closed. I opened my eyes. It doesn't matter. I could bark, I suppose. Specific moments last longer. I'm delaying, waiting for something. The light is softer. I might have been waiting for the light to become softer.

The door opened.

I was waiting for the door to open.

An old man with small pale blue eyes peers in at me. He wears a dirty white captain's hat, a black turtle-neck jersey and cowboy chaps. His sockless feet are covered by unlaced army-surplus shoes. He points a pistol at me.

"You'd be old Lockett's boy? Fashioned after him. Been twenty years or more since I last laid eyes on him. Killed hisself running after a freight, if I recall."

His face is thin and hard. A short white beard struggles across his chin.

"You coming out, or do I have to make you come on out? Locketts always was ornery."

I came out. He put the pistol inside his belt. Meridith leans against a fender. She seems younger. She has managed to wash her face and put on fresh make-up.

"I can't get him to drive, Captain," she says. "He's completely shiftless. All he thinks about is this crazy plan of his."

"Like his pappy." The captain looks through the door into the camper. "Ought to brand his ass a little. Locketts always did need a push. Always getting trapped by fool schemes."

The sun has disappeared. The sky is bloody and violent. I have seen all that before. A red adobe stands on a slight rise surrounded by gray sage. Black mountains circle us. The skeletons of four cars and a truck lie on the side of the road. The captain walks away, behind the adobe. Meridith and I followed.

"I got fifteen hundred for the camper and everything in it," Meridith whispered to me. "Plus an old pickup to get us there."

We found the captain lifting a long pole into a slat set in a post. The fence stretches completely around the adobe. It is a high three-poled fence.

"No time to jaw," the captain said. "Got to get this together inside a fortnight. Flash flood coming on. Got the only water hole for ten miles around. They never stop trying to get at it. I seen you coming for two mile. Had you lined up every square inch of the way. Takin no chances. Seen you done some shooting not too long back. Noticed your empties on the floor."

I helped him lift a pole into another slat.

"Respect a man that comes up with a plan and sticks to it. Never mind about your pappy. Figure you heard about me from him. More to say but you ain't about to step inside my door. People step all over you first chance they get. Nobody been in my place for six years or more. Plenty to do. If it ain't one thing it's another. Coyotes after the milk cows. Sandstorms. Government on you all the time about signing fool papers. Never signed nothing. Cattle charge through from time to time. Seen an airplane crash oncet about five miles south."

He rolls himself a smoke. It is night. Meridith sits on a pile of fence posts, her head in her hand.

"Too dark to keep working," the captain said. "But many a time I worked straight on through to the dawn. Got me a good perimeter worked out. Three hundred yards outside the fence got a barbwire arrangement with cans tied on, dynamite planted. Got rocks piled up to stop vehicles coming through. Rocks give a good line of fire. Extended the wash back of the house. Got tunnels going in and out. Figure to drag them automobiles over one of these days. Start another wall. Pour cement into em."

Meridith stood up.

"We have to move on. We have to be there in ten hours."

The cigarette fell from the captain's lips. He grinds it out with his heel. He looks at us shrewdly. "Got a working mine, but I ain't sure exactly where it is. Found it some twenty years ago. Stole machinery. Figure to work it one of these days. I could give you a piece of that. But don't get ideas. Come back easy like. Rustlers took to roping off a few calves one year. Shot two of em. Drillers came soon after. Punched holes in the ground. Dynamited them and their machines."

The captain walked back to the adobe and shut the door.

We followed the dirt road back to the camper. Meridith took out the bag and a bottle of gin. A rifle swivels back and forth from a window in the adobe. The stars . . . no, I've forgotten the stars. Nog is crouched in the corner of a living room with only a tee shirt on. He stares at a large-boned woman in an evening gown reading a fashion magazine. We turned off into a shallow wash where we found a blue Chevy pickup truck with Illinois plates. Meridith lifted up the hood and deftly took out a time bomb attached to the starter. She put the bag in the back and climbed in behind the wheel. I'm staying outside. I don't want to go inside. It's too close. The seats are cracked brown leather, and there is a horseshoe nailed to the dashboard. Meridith must have put the bomb into the bag before she threw it in the back. It was very small. The motor has started. She's turning around. I was aware of no hunch about myself, so I got in. We drove down the dirt road and onto the highway. I leaned my head back on the seat and shut my eyes. I can feel Meridith unzip my fly with one hand and slowly caress my cock.

I must have fallen asleep. We're in a city or we're approaching a city. We might be on a thruway. Headlights flash by. My head is in Meridith's lap. Her right thigh is over my neck. The back of my head rests against her left thigh. My nose presses against her cunt. What is this about a plan? I can see her chin between her perfect breasts. Her lips appear thoughtful and set in a firm line. Her nostrils are nicely turned. I can't see her eyes. It's not important to see her eyes. It's enough to feel her breathe evenly, to match my rise and fall with her rise and fall. Locked together, we're moving forward even while motionless. What do I need Nog for, buried within the odors of a plan. He's trying to hitchhike, but no one stops for him. He'll go anywhere, east or west. But he's moving east.

"L.A.," Meridith said.

I tried. Or I think I tried to get back into the land. Was that what I was trying to do, to inhabit the land? There is New York, where I first started. I'm not as fast now. Memories are slower, fewer, although there is still a necessity to invent something to put together. I might be traveling in an arc, like a half-moon, or perhaps a circle to the full moon. I could close the arc by streaking back. It's too soon to invent anything about the desert. I know there was a clearing in the woods, and before that I helped repair a boarding house. That's all very clear. I painted and arranged rooms for my board. That's good enough. That works. That sounds acceptable.

"We're early," Meridith said. "It's not light yet. We'll get rid of the truck and walk in."

I haven't tried hard enough. There was a storm. I can always start with that. I lost something. I lost an octopus. That separation had nothing to do with islands or beaches. I might as well get straight about that.

"We're in Long Beach," Meridith said.

A drift has been halted, now that there is a plan. There's no denying that. I'm steadier now, more relaxed, calmer certainly and more direct. My Stetson has kept its shape. It must be in the back, next to the bag, or on top of the bag.

I sat up.

Oil drills slowly buck into the ground. There are lights, palm trees and ranch-style houses. We're crossing a bridge or an overpass. We're downtown. There are tall buildings, stores, hotels and bars. That's enough description. Who cares anyway? It's either very late or very early in the morning. Meridith parked the truck.

"We can walk from here," she said. "We have an hour to waste."

I don't like to just park a truck and walk away. I've done that before. I need to linger. Meridith took the bag, and I took the Stetson. Another part of the brim has been cut off. I sat on the hood of the truck. Then I kicked each of the tires and got in and out of the front seat. Anything to waste time. Meridith stares at shoes in a store window. Sailors pass. Meridith follows them. I'm following Meridith. I can smell the sea. We're probably heading towards the sea. We stepped off the curb and crossed the street to an amusement park. Rides still operate, but lights are slowly winking off. A few people linger by the hot-dog stands. There are no barkers. Meridith follows the sailors, although now there are only two. Her ankles are slender, even elegant. Her feet don't point to the right or left. A sailor has stopped in front of a tattoo parlor. Meridith stops and I stop. The sailor put a long arm around Meridith, drawing her to him. She kissed him and whispered something in his ear. He gravely walks away.

We went into the tattoo parlor.

Colored photographs of tattoos cover the walls. An old man sits in a blue director's chair. He wears sandals, red-and-white-striped linen overalls and a blue work shirt. Dark glasses wrap around his eyes. His face is emaciated. He has no hair. On his sallow cheek a rhinoceros charges towards his tight-lipped mouth.

"Got yourself half an hour," he said.

A low counter separates the waiting room from the

operation room, where there are three sets of needles.

"You tell him what to do to me," Meridith said. "I'll tell him what to do to you." She whispered in his ear. He nods slowly. Then she sat down.

"A map of the U.S. on her ass," I whispered into his flaky ear. "But don't put any ink in the needle." I sat down on a chair.

"The wife will help," the man said. "You ain't got but half an hour. Both of you drop your pants and lean over the counter."

We dropped our pants to our ankles and leaned over the counter. A ferris wheel revolves outside. There are a few lights and then darkness. The darkness must be the sea.

My ass is being punctured. Perhaps this is part of the plan. Meridith reaches out to hold my hand. In front of us, blocking out the lower curve of the ferris wheel, are five faces pushing their noses and lips to the windowpane. The smashed features all look the same. The bodies are young and dressed in two mini skirts, a bikini and two pairs of white chino pants. There are no shoes.

"Don't look at your ass for a few weeks," Meridith said. "Try to hold out."

There is no way to tell if the man or the woman is working on my ass. Meridith gazes fondly at me. I don't want to look at her. I can't look at the faces or the bodies pressed against the window. My ass hurts. I am able to look at the photographs on the wall.

"If this works out we might be home for Christmas," Meridith said. "But I don't know why I get myself into these painful situations."

She rubs my arm lightly with her fingers. Her touch is painful. It's almost possible to look at the top of the ferris wheel.

"You need a bath," Meridith said. Her voice has become quicker and slightly hysterical. "You need to get yourself sharpened up. You're a slob. I'm so utterly exhausted, traveling around, smelling you, hearing you continually bitch, watching you spill your food, seeing you ruin everything, missing every cue, every nuance, every connection, every onc-liner, every turnoff, every gas station, every direction. And my ass is hurting. What did you tell him to put on it? My ass isn't all that big or important. I'm sick of not having a decent change of underwear, of dirty fingernails, of fucking in the sand, of eating out of cans, of not having enough make-up, of irregular hours."

She is crying. Her hand grips my wrist.

"Oh, darling. I don't know what to do. I'm so confused. That's not true. I have the tickets. We'll go on. Something will work out . . . You're so sweet. So well-intentioned."

The faces have changed. They've floated away. The faces were gone a long time ago. But they were definitely there, if only for a few minutes. Nog too has been lined up, his face smashed against the window. But it doesn't work with him. He rushes up too fast, throws himself down, forgets himself and then, when you least expect it, he's gone. I don't know what to do about him. I've obviously goofed. But I'm stuck. It might have been better to have kept adding to the list. Lists don't need directions. I don't regret Nog, or at least having met him. I want to say that now, before he does himself in. It's necessary to have a name, a face to fill in the empty spaces, a voice for the silences, to keep going when you don't know if you're going on or not. It's a matter of addition and subtraction. His blank eyes will hit the other side of the country and then automatically turn back. The needles have stopped.

We pulled up our pants. Meridith paid from a huge wad of bills she pulled from her pocket. We left without seeing the man's wife.

The lights have gone out in the amusement park. We walked through it and crossed a bridge spanning a muddy canal. It is dawn. An oil drill nods into the ground. Nothing else moves. We move. We're moving on. Piles of rubble stretch away on both sides of the road. There are no more oil drills. I can smell the sea again. Red lights on two radio towers blink on and off. I first talked with Nog in such a ravaged and raped landscape. It is a battlefield of bricks, oil cans, skeletons and rubble of shacks, rimless tires, piles of garbage, smashed iceboxes and smoked glass. We're approaching a long cement dock and the outlines of two ships. Yellow fork-lifts back in and out of a tin shed. A freighter is being loaded. I have to sit down.

I sat on the curb. It is very painful. Meridith walked on a few feet. She looks towards the sea.

Nog has to be warmer, more immediate. I have to know every feature, every inflection, every gesture, every desire, every hurt before he slips away, before I lose him. That's impossible. He doesn't do his share. He doesn't expose himself enough. Perhaps I've made too many demands. Perhaps he has come to despise me. There are other memories pressing, but Nog has to be confronted before I can move on.

"I'm your sister," Meridith said. She stands beside me. I put an arm around her leg. "Lockett is tattooed on your ass, in case you forget. I wasn't going to tell you, but it doesn't matter."

I stood up. She handed me a ticket. We walked to the dock and stood before the ship. Green paint peels off her sides. *The Buffalo* is printed on her bow.

We sat on a wooden bench. The last fork-lift disappeared into the shed. A few sailors move about the bow. A cook dumps garbage over the stern. He leans on the railing, looking down at the water. The captain paces the bridge.

"We have a few minutes," Meridith said.

Finger Lakes, Lake Tahoe, Lake Louise, Lake Geneva, Whiskey Lake, Lake Winnepega. I've never been to any of those lakes.

"We have to go," Meridith said. She's squeezing my hand. I don't feel like looking at her. I haven't felt like looking at her for the last hour. If only a voice, this distance, this voice, would stop. The water doesn't lap. The sea is out there, waiting. I have done that before. The captain yells, pointing at us.

We stood up. Meridith took my hand and we walked to the gangplank. We must have left something behind. Meridith has the bag, I have the Stetson, but something has been left behind. Or perhaps it is because nothing has been left behind, nothing abandoned. There's an emptiness, but there's always an emptiness. No comfort there.

"The Locketts?" The captain leans over the bridge,

peering down at us. He has a small and pinched weather-beaten face. I can't distinguish any more than that.

"We're the Locketts," Meridith said.

"You have exactly three and one half minutes to board this ship. We sail at six thirty-seven. Not six thirty-six or six thirty-eight. At six thirty-seven my men throw over the ropes, the tug comes and we're moving. The steward will show you to your quarters."

He walked into the chart room. Meridith is tired. She gave me her ticket and we went up the gangplank. I handed the tickets to the steward. We followed him to Meridith's cabin on the port side. Then I followed the steward to my cabin on the starboard side. I can only see water through the porthole. I pulled the curtain. The cabin is neat and compact. It's a relief, I suppose, to pass out in a cabin.

I'M cold. Or I was cold. I might be approaching a warmth. I don't remember when I've last fallen asleep in a warm bath. There is a slight rocking. I am probably awake. I met Meridith in a warm bath. I followed her down metal steps to a darkly lit room with a round ceiling. One wall was an aquarium. We undressed each other . . . It's difficult to manage a decent erection in the morning. Either that or it's too easy. In the middle of the room, on a small platform, there was a huge mollusk or conch shell. The shell existed on different levels. The water was gently perfumed. I sat on a shelf opposite and slightly above her.

My skin relaxed and seemed to float gently over the rest of me . . . That is vast enough. That helps a little. But I have yet to exert myself. I'm like a slug building its house and fortress out of its own saliva. The inside of me is becoming a swelling assemblage of shells. My cock is a fossil, but not merely a being that has once lived, but one still active, asleep but rousing now to its own form. A water phoenix subject to resurrection . . . The shell has floated away, leaving the hum that comes vibrating down miles and miles of spirals.

I should look around.

Where is the bag? The bag is not in the center of the cabin. I had thought of the bag as being in the center of the cabin. I don't remember how I got here . . . Meridith must have shoved me in. The cabin is small and compact. There is blue sky out the porthole. Meridith calmed my fears. Either that or I calmed her fears. She came back to tuck me in and, leaning down, sucked me into place. Meridith must have the bag. I should have listed the physical aspects of the desert, the colors that related to thoughts. Hunger as flat orange became sienna. Purple and fear as it dissolved to black. But I don't need a list now. I need the bag. I was doing well enough until I stumbled on the octopus in the middle of the saloon. I can't stop remembering. At first it was a cactus, but looking back, I can remember the little beak nose and the rubbery arms. Lockett was responsible for that. I should remember Lockett. I should invent him more. I should depend on the attachment that comes with distance. But there is no time. I need the bag. Meridith might have left the ship. If Meridith is gone the bag will relieve me. It will be a relief to dump out the contents and put them back in again, to add to them, I might shove the contents over the side. It doesn't matter. I want the bag. It might be evening. The light is soft. But I can't look out the porthole. I am beginning to remember. There was Lockett's sermon in the saloon. He never got started. I staked out a claim while waiting for Nog. I have begun to smell his fear. He is stinking up the cabin while he crosses the Hudson River.

I swung my feet out enough to face the sink. That was an hour ago. I slipped into blue jeans and tee shirt and stole into an alleyway. I am crouched there now. Two seamen have passed. The alleyway is freshly painted. I have been in alley- and passageways before. I'm either going to step out on deck or turn to the right, down another alleyway. It is too clean and airy here. There is no place to sit down or rest. People stride through as if they have someplace to go. If I move I might stumble into a connection, I might be able to reach out for the bag. A bell chimed four times.

I stepped outside.

I can smell the sea. The sky rolls over me. I can't look. I ran to the railing and threw up. The icy wake bubbles, and the blue is deeper near the side. I'm lying on a hatch cover. The sky and salt air pinion me to the canvas. My skin is not enough protection. The ship makes no noise as it moves either north or south or east.

I stepped inside.

I took eight steps down an alleyway and opened a

heavy door. I am on a metal landing above the engine room. The heat is dry and the engines throb quietly. I have forgotten the sharp cut of the bow. I climbed down the steep ladder to a lower level. The soles of my boots are thin, and my feet burn. Two firemen stand before their instruments. They're dressed in white coveralls. They have long gloves, and the backs of their necks are pale. I can't see their faces. The heat is more intense. I am only able to remember my cabin and the white enamel sink. I've forgotten what it is that I'm looking for. I might remember if I could lie down in front of a boiler. Organs would pop. My skin would fry. I could brand my tongue on the side of the boiler. I would either remember it all or never have to again. There are levels beneath this one. A wiper climbs silently by me, carrying a bucket of oil. I have the strength to descend. A man stands on a platform ten feet away. His lips are moving and he is smiling. Either that or he is scowling. He wears blue coveralls and white canvas shoes. His body is erect and his face sags into hundreds of wrinkles around his mouth and chin. I don't want to notice him any more. He has already gotten in the way. I am being pulled down to the bottom level. But I can't move. There is nothing down there anyway. There is always something above and something below no matter where you're standing. The heat, if nothing else, drove me to the top.

I walked across an alleyway and leaned my head against a bulkhead. I must slow down. I must let it form slowly. It is happening, but I must watch it happen.

An officer approaches. I entered a cabin before I could see more than his white hat.

"Is that you, dearie?"

The shrill voice comes from behind a screen. The screen is pasted with magazine cutouts of movie stars. There are two round and faded yellow rugs and a small desk lacquered Chinese red. An orange cat sleeps on a yellow chaise lounge. Potted ferns hang from hooks on the ceiling. The cabin is larger than mine. It must be a stateroom.

"Come closer." The voice is shrill and impatient.

I looked behind the screen. A small pale face with huge circular brown eyes is centered in the middle of a blue satin pillow. The double bed is a bronze four-poster. The face has high cheek bones and thin blue hair. The thin mouth is firmly closed. Most of the face has been covered with thick make-up, the eyes circled crudely with charcoal.

"I heard five bells," she says. "Supper is at six bells. You're too early."

I walked over to the porthole. I'm in no special hurry. The portholes are covered with thick paper or cardboard. They have been painted over with sparkling blue waves, jumping dolphins and lavender skies. Her voice comes in gasps.

"The Caribbean . . . the Canal . . . thirty-three . . . eighty-eight times . . . Culebra Cut . . ."

I sat down in a wicker rocking chair. I rock towards her. There is no indication of a body underneath the brown blankets. Her lips are smeared with orange lipstick. A plastic gold star has been pasted just off the center of her forehead.

"You must be the new radio operator. You don't look like a cook."

The officer must have passed through the alleyway by now. He didn't follow me. He might not have noticed me. A bony hand grips my wrist.

"Are we in a storm? Tell me the truth, baby. I won't stand being lied to any more. I feel this frightful rocking. We will have to put out a sheet anchor to keep us heading into the wind. We've weathered storms before. We'll survive. Send this message: 'Rough weather but pleasant company.' "

She opened her thin lips and attempted a toothless smile. I can manage looking at the porthole over her head.

"The storm will continue," I said. "There is no sign of a letup. The barometer, however, is steady. There is no panic aboard. We are getting closer all the time."

She isn't listening. She has shut her eyes and is sucking her lips in and out. Her hand still grips my wrist even though I haven't stopped rocking.

"Where is the girl?" she asked.

"I don't know," I said.

"She's adorable. She never speaks. The needle goes in so gently I never feel a thing. That's hard with veins like mine. She's better than the steward. His teeth are so rotten and yellow. I'm grateful we managed to procure her. Send a message to that effect. It's been years since anything so beautiful has come through that door."

Her grip relaxed and she patted my hand. I withdrew it.

"I hate to break in a new man," she snarled. "Slip into a yellow robe. You'll find it in the closet."

Meridith has been here, working out with the bag. I must get to the bag before she has too much of a claim on it. But I need to be released from here. I'm unable to just walk out. Perhaps the robe will be a catalyst.

I left the door of the closet half open for light and because the smell of jasmine is too overpowering. I counted eighteen robes in various sizes. From three yellow robes I chose the largest. It's comforting in here. I could get used to the jasmine.

"Don't sniff through my uniforms forever, baby."

I slipped on the yellow robe over my clothes and walked over to the rocking chair.

"On the floor," she ordered. "Drop your pants and fold them neatly. They're horrid. I wouldn't want to know what you've been doing in them. Now get into position in the middle of that round rug. That's a good boy."

I am sitting on the floor in the middle of a round rug. I can't see her face, only her hand clawing the side of the bed. But now she has propped herself up, revealing a high-necked black nightgown.

"Show me the message. I don't have all day. And don't sit. Didn't they tell you anything? Kneel towards the door."

My ass points towards the bed. I am prostrating myself, my arms in front of me.

"I've traveled over a thousand miles," I said.

"Yes, yes," she said. "I know all that."

I have to say something. I have to give out with

some information. She must want to know about Meridith.

"Meridith never speaks," I said. "It is her silence that holds me. The only relief comes from touching her, from rubbing a hand across her stomach."

My robe has been slowly raised.

"We studied natural life; fauna, octopi, rocks, shells . . . I have to find her. She has something that I need. I can describe her to you. She has a smooth back, soft down on the inside of her thighs . . ."

I am not saying the right words. The robe is now over my back.

"Her legs are long and rubbery, like tentacles. We have traveled the length of highways together, climbed mountains, crossed deserts, floated down rivers . . . Her mouth is soft. Her eyes never focus when you speak directly to her. I don't know where she's from . . ."

The robe covers me again. I am still kneeling towards the door.

"I never crossed over a lake with her. I've never been in a park with her. We never investigated coves or harbors. We don't know anything about birds. She is always distant but always within reach. We have shared corners, campers, back seats, hallways and bathtubs. She smells like fresh hay. She can be moist if you have the patience to find the right spot. I was breathing in and out, just getting through the golden days, when she walked by the window. Her ankles were so thin. I followed them into the mountains and down into the desert . . ."

Snores stopped me. She is asleep, her head turned towards the wall. I stood up.

"It is all right," she said, opening her eyes. "My darling Lockett. At last. Lockett. Lockett. Take good care of her."

I left the cabin.

I need to see land. I rushed for a porthole. Nothing on the starboard side. A bell chimes six times. I ran on deck. There is a smudge on the port side. Land. We are heading south.

"Get out of that goddamn robe," the captain yells from the bridge. I retraced my steps.

She is still awake. "Don't worry, dear Lockett." Her eyes close but her hand grips mine. "Everything will resolve itself. We'll come together again. You'll see. Sweet boy. We'll join hands in front of the icebox late at night. Remember . . . the loud hymns, the games . . . ? I haven't been off this ship in eight years. She must have told you . . . He always tried not to let us sail too far from land. He's a good captain. We circle the continent. A coastal freighter. Citrus fruit, salt. Harmless . . . When he has to cross over to another ocean he waits for night. He's so considerate. He makes sure I never know . . . You'll learn to be proud of him."

She is asleep. Or she is resting. Her mouth is half open. I bent closer, enough to see the large loose pores in her skin.

I changed into my pants. I wonder where my Stetson is. But it is my stomach I must tend to. I can't afford too many aching cavities. I walked down the alleyway. At the end, as I had hoped, was the dining room. It is clean and cheerful, with blue curtains over the portholes. The long table is covered by a spotless white tablecloth. Paintings of sailing ships decorate the walls. The captain enters. He is shorter than I had imagined, his face stern and impassive. Meridith follows with a tray and places shrimp cocktails before us. I sit at the far end of the table, opposite the captain. There are other place mats, but no one occupies them. Meridith never looks at me. She wears a nurse's uniform with white stockings and white shoes. Her hair has been pulled into a neat bun.

The captain speaks. "We were eight minutes early getting into port. Every clock is uncoordinated. When I call for speed I want speed. And when I want to slow down I want to slow down. I want to rub against that dock at four thirty-seven P.M., not four fifty-six P.M. And when the bell strikes six I don't want to wait. I want you in here."

His brow furrows—his mouth becoming slack, almost uncontrolled.

"Getting in and out fouls everything. I plan for days. Don't want to waste time in port. Haven't been off this ship in . . . it will be eight years, three months and seven days."

I nodded over a spoon of soup.

"I know you've been messing around on the land. I want no part of it. Never tell me. . . . We should enter the Canal tomorrow at four forty-six P.M. That's all I'm required to tell you."

Meridith hands the captain three pills. She watches him swallow them and then returns to the galley.

"Pass Bona Island two or three minutes past three

P.M. Never had any use for islands. Figure I should inform you of what's going on, even though you never took the trouble to inform me."

The soup has been followed by roast beef, mashed potatoes and string beans. The captain lifts his eyes to the ceiling. His voice lowers.

"The main thing," he says, "is to be obedient for a long time, and in one and the same direction. Keep to the same space. Don't try to go to new ports. Eight hundred Chinese were imported to build a railroad alongside the Canal. They committed suicide when they were deprived of their opium. They strangled or hanged themselves or sat down on the beach and waited for the tide to drown them. Let that be a lesson to you. Be kind to her."

I'm not hungry. There is no sign of Meridith.

The captain stands, throwing his napkin on the table.

"You never did listen to anything," he said. "You never asked for anything. Always smug. Always feeling sorry for yourself."

I am alone. I must be waiting for Meridith. But I have been sitting here for an hour and she hasn't appeared. The mess boy cleared the table. If I only knew exactly what to think over, what information to digest. It's night. I can glimpse darkness through a slit in the curtain.

I walked down the alleyway and onto the deck. I'm lying on a hatch amidships. Men drift by on either side. Someone plays an harmonica. The sea is black and silent. It is cooler. I have been in and out of harbors: Cork, Barcelona, Liverpool, Copenhagen, Atlanta, New Orleans, Ceuta, Port Said, Calcutta, Hong Kong, Philadelphia, Singapore, Boston, Acapulco, Rio, Port Arthur, Hoboken and Sydney. I don't remember San Francisco or Le Havre. I added and subtracted a few harbors, making the list more bearable. Nog has found his way from one harbor to another. He might not be perverse enough to make it back. He panhandles, saving money for a bus to Santa Fe. He might be going back. Everything depends on him going back. He has almost OD'd, has been busted and is out on probation, has tried to jump off the Manhattan bridge, has fucked three celebrities and has passed out in the subway entrance at Delancey Street. There is only a slit now for Nog. He hides in Central Park. I have never trusted parks. I have never made a list of parks. He buries his sleeping bag by day and drags it out at night. He sleeps near a stagnant pond. He has given up watching children sail rubber boats.

I must have fallen asleep because the stars have shifted. I'm on my back, but I won't mention the stars any more. A small pinpoint of light flows on the starboard side. No one drifts by. I can't hear the sea, but I can sense the waves undulating and swelling. A bell chimed twice and I sat up.

Meridith sits cross-legged before a kerosene lamp. Two flying fish lie at her feet. I sit beside her. Her right hand rests on top of the bag. My Stetson balances on her kneecap.

"Flying fish are attracted to the light," she said. "He likes them for breakfast."

She looks ahead, at the black waves. But she must

know I'm sitting beside her. She must have stolen a glance as I crept over. Surely she's capable of that.

"In the Indian Ocean we used to get a lot. They'd swarm up in bunches. I used to lie on deck and let them fall on me. Sometimes we used to all do it together."

"I want to ask you something," I said.

"We're somewhere near the Humboldt Current," she said quietly. Her eyes have never left the black waves. "Off Peru the Humboldt meets with another current and there are huge sea monsters. One night a giant squid reached up and pulled down a small fishing boat. The squid was attracted to the light. Two men drowned."

The fish are blue and green. Their gills are still moving in and out. I put on the Stetson. The bag is next to me. Perhaps I wanted to ask her about the bag. But it doesn't matter. We're all together again.

Nothing flies towards us from the sea. Meridith touched my hand.

"The bag is full now," she said.

Her eyes are heavy-lidded. Her fingers preoccupied and absent. It is as if she is full as well. She is barefoot, and a green tee shirt hangs over her jeans. Her hair is loose over her shoulders. A flying fish lands in front of us. She hands me a small white pill. She watches me carefully.

"I have never given you anything before," I said.

"Thank you," she said softly. "It will be an offering."

The dim outline of the captain slowly paces back

and forth on the bridge, stopping at each end to peer towards us.

"He has never seen me make it with anyone," Meridith said. "Not you, anyway."

The pill rests in the palm of my hand. Meridith's hand rests lightly on the end of my cock.

"It will put you out," she said.

There must have been something Lockett was trying to tell me, trying to prepare me for. I can't remember the sound of his voice. I have to begin. His voice was low and coarse. I met him in a rooming house outside of a large industrial city. We shared meals. He had a lean flat-nosed face . . . Meridith has unzipped my fly. Her hand darts inside my pants, gathering my cock and balls together. My cock presses against her closed fingers. She slowly widens them, letting me burst forth. With her other hand she takes the pill and places it on the tip of her tongue. She inserted her tongue into my mouth and shoved the pill down my throat.

"It is just that there is so much to do tonight," she whispered.

"What is there to do?" I asked. I have never asked anything of her before.

Before her mouth devours my cock I want to say something. There should be something to say, about her, about me . . . The captain paces on the bridge. I am on my back once more. Her hand slowly rubs my stomach. My Stetson has fallen over my eyes.

"I've been traveling about the West," I said. But that isn't true. I don't know how to move on. What is it that she wants? If I knew that. I should say that.

"I'll help you with your rounds," I said. "I tried to

tell you on the river we were floating down a river together. I've had my eye on you. Perhaps that's it. I don't blame myself for that . . . There was a moment in the bathtub when I made a move towards you. There were other, smaller gestures. I never made the mistake of considering you. I'm fading . . . I must have gathered something together back there without knowing it . . ."

A fish slaps on the deck. Then another. The flapping is louder. We must have sliced through a school. Let them come. Let them flap to death near the light. I'm bursting now . . .

The sun streams through. I'm warm. Or I was warm. I might be approaching a coolness. I don't remember when I've last fallen asleep in a cold bath. The ship is still. I am probably awake. I first noticed Meridith floating down a wide river. At first the river was silent but then it moaned and I have an erection and it was as if we were talking to each other. We bumped through the rapids. The river curved and then straightened. I don't want anything to happen. The inside of me is full of grinding shells. My cock is no longer a fossil, no longer asleep. It has resurrected.

I don't need to look around. I know the bag isn't in the middle of the cabin.

I ran up on deck. I must be looking for the bag. There is no sign of it. We're passing a small brown island on the port side. Gannets fly over the bow and dive straight down for the flying fish. A porpoise slaps the water. The sky is heavy and overcast. The captain paces the bridge, looking neither to the right nor left.

We're passing another island, and the sea has become a shallow green.

I ran below. I remember the alleyway. I remember this door and the old woman. It is coming back. I tried the handle to her door. It is locked. I called out softly. No one answers. I knocked. No one answers. I kicked at the door. Then I walked back down the alleyway, crossed quickly over to another alleyway and found my own cabin. I am beginning to inhabit this space. Alleyways are no problem. The cabin is clean and the bed made. I threw water on my face from the sink. There is no sign of Meridith or the bag. I had thought they might be curled up together on the bed. I ran on deck.

Fourteen pelicans fly over the bow in tight formation. We're passing *The Moise*, a tanker sunk low in the water. The huge space is in back of us. The sun sinks. The captain paces to the edge of the bridge and disappears into the chart room. I don't want to look at the approach to the Canal. I'm no good at approaches. I would attempt a look from the stern, at the last sweep of sky, but the pilot boat has come alongside. There are too many details. Another list is starting. I am unable to avoid it, as if the space has caused me to shrink back and expand into detail at the same time. I am sliding from one ocean to another and the slide is taking over, the slide within and without. It is too hot to hide in the engine room. My cabin is too clean and empty. I have to make it on deck. I have to find the bag. I can't remember Nog or Lockett or both of them together. Not now. That is changing. I don't want to be particular. It's not possible to make a list. It is being done for me. It is all around me. Meridith must be hiding. I need to find her. Is that going forward or backward? The more I need to touch her and the bag, to feel the tentacles of a plan, the more immobile I become . . . A rusty Greek freighter. I counted twenty-eight portholes. A German freighter anchored to port. We're poking into the hot opening. A battered World War II seaplane and Navy quarters with red-tiled roofs. We're slipping inside. It happened easily enough. A minimum of panting and greasing. The sailors go about their business. They've gone both ways before, from one tide to another, one sea to another, through the land. My voice fumbles. I need the bag. A Navy LST appears behind us, blocking the Pacific. Soldiers in fatigues wave towards the shore, and above glide hundreds of gulls and one lone frigate bird. We're inside the slit now. No turning back. Nothing for it but to plunge on to the manufactured end. The Pacific is gone.

Round hills burned off and a Japanese freighter of the Mitsui Line. It is darker, more humid. Sea smell is gone. We are under a bridge full of new cars. A child waves. I lay down on a hatch. Meridith was just someone that fell into town. Her function as a mother and sister and to whom is not my problem, even if it has become my problem. My breath has thickened. I can't remember her. I would probably recognize her mouth. The eyes are vague, possibly green, but the hair is no problem. A dyed blond. The ankles aren't as thin as I first thought. They're fat and bulky. I can't hear the sound of her voice.

I was rescued by sitting up and red buoys bobbing.

A dense green presses in on both sides. Sounds of birds and a yellow canary flying across the bow. I must have moved up to the bow because I'm sitting up there, on top of the initial thrust, watching a helicopter and *The Karenmata* out of Amsterdam and then a beautiful schooner, *The Blue Moon*. Radio towers, derricks, barges and more barracks. A field of washing machines and iceboxes. The lines were joined on the river. I was unaware of the sides, only the flow ahead. The camper was restful, and there were moments on the ledge when I felt at ease. The car was uncomfortable, and the hospital strained and hysterical. That takes care of that. I was morose in the bathtub. I'm frightened in stationary water. But the lake was wonderful. I remember the calm lake and the cranes flying overhead and the soft slap of the oars and my hand on her breast. It was either early evening or dawn. It is almost dark. We're approaching a lock. Miraflores. 1913. A bell chimes. The captain is nowhere to be seen. A large green neon arrow points us towards the lock. Electric mules, like little railroad engines, three on each side, tow us through. It is true that I am riding something out. The workers have blue-and-green and blue-and-white helmets. I can hear crickets. We ascend fifty-four feet through double locks in ten minutes. Information is written on the sides of the lock. I can look forward and towards both sides at once. On the bridge, the pilot directs the mules, waving his hands in signals. A man has come out of the control tower. He might be looking at me. But he hasn't responded to my wave. Everyone is focused on their own task.

On the poop deck there is no sign of Meridith.

Night has fallen. Lights glow every fifty feet from steel poles. A half sunken sailboat and flames where they're burning back the jungle. Going through San Pedro Lock, I saw Meridith sitting in a lifeboat on the other side of the poop deck. She appears to be looking at me. A low humming comes out of the jungle.

"It's the Cut now," she said.

I climbed into the lifeboat and sat on the seat opposite her. We held each other's hands. A ship glides silently past.

"I'm afraid," she said.

A faint clicking from the jungle. A ship passes with sailors dancing from a radio on one of the hatches.

"I gave you the best years of my life, Lockett."

A concrete dock to starboard and the frames of steel buildings lit up.

"What will I do if the directions aren't right, if I don't have the right information?"

A blinking green light along the starboard edge.

"You understand the situation, don't you, Lockett? You've always understood, isn't that right?"

A wire fence surrounding radio towers. Then another ship. Red lights blink.

"I knew you would come through for me the first time I saw you. I've stolen notes of yours. I tore some up and put the ones that are readable in the bag. That's how much I love you."

Rain makes it impossible to distinguish the sides of the Canal.

She squeezes my hand. "Meet me when we anchor at Gatun Lake. On the port side in thirty minutes."

She climbed out of the lifeboat, reaching back to

take the bag from underneath the seat. She is gone. The bag is gone with her. I should move on. But I'm doing nicely in the lifeboat. Nog hasn't found a way out of Central Park. He has been there for a week. He has accosted several children. He has enough to eat from handouts and minor thefts, but he has had to move his sleeping bag several times.

I left the lifeboat. I'm in the alleyway, pounding on the old woman's door.

"You ought to see this," I yelled. "Everything is managed. Pilots direct everything."

I can barely hear her voice.

"Thirty-six . . . through again . . . no time . . . all those boys . . . Lockett . . . Please . . . Please . . ."

Her voice stopped. I can hear no sound within. An engineer in white coveralls passes, puffing on a cigar. I went on deck.

The rain is harder. We have stopped moving. We must be in a lake. There is a faint glow ahead, as if from a distant city. The captain came out of the chart room, looked around and went back in again. I can see the silhouettes of eleven ships anchored near us. We must be waiting in line to go through the final lock. The rain is warm. Meridith walks across the deck, dragging a small rubber boat and a black bag. She is dressed in a rubber wet suit.

"You don't have to get in the water," she said. "I'll tow you across. I've already blown up the boat. When I get in, throw the bag and the paddle down."

There is already a rope ladder over the side. She puts together a red plastic paddle. Bells chime. I missed dinner. No one is about, and the bridge remains empty. There are no signals, no blinking lights from the other ships. Meridith flung her arms around me.

"I'm so afraid," she said. Her arms are rubbery and hard. She presses against me in the sticky rain. She is trying to drag me into the boat, although we haven't moved. I put my arms around her. She stepped back and looked at me quizzically. I am unable to cope with quizzical glances.

I handed the paddle to her, but she handed it back.

"When I get in the boat, darling, hand the paddle and the bag to me."

When she was on the last rung of the ladder, I dropped the rubber boat into the black oily water. She hooked it to her with her foot and got in. In her wet suit, it is hard to distinguish if she is a man or a woman.

"I can't do it alone," she said finally, looking up at me.

She appears to be pouting.

"You don't understand what we have to do," she said. "You don't understand what it involves."

I handed her the paddle. She grips it, but I am unable to let it go.

"There's more than one person involved," she pleaded.

I tugged at the paddle, but she holds firm.

"You can't desert me," she said angrily.

I pulled at the paddle, and this time it came back.

"At least hand me the bag," she demanded. "I can't do anything without the bag."

But the bag remains between my feet. It is raining

harder. I sat down and reached into the bag. I took out a vial of pills and took five of them, letting the rest drop to the deck.

"Hand me the bag," she ordered.

I lay down and leaned my head against the bag. I spoke softly.

"I don't know if I can remember anyone who is apart from me for very long."

The ship started suddenly to move. She tried to grab the ladder, but it is too late. She is weeping. I am probably weeping.

"Not yet," she yells. "No . . . No . . . No . . . No . . ."

She drifts away from the stern. The captain appears on the bridge. He stares at the ship's wake.

"There's no current," she yelled.

She has faded into the rain and the shadow of a huge tanker.

"The boat is leaking. Nog, the boat leaks. Lockett. Daddy. Stop."

The ship gains speed. We're being processed through Gatun Lock. Mules answer the pilot's signals with streetcar bells: ding, ding . . .

We're sinking from one ocean to another. There are three ships now in three different locks on three different levels. There is a ship below us and a ship above us. Red and green lights blink on and off. I am able to concentrate on the names written on the sides of the locks: Mathew Luckenback. Henry Salte. Marty. Regina. Norman. David. Kurt. Lefty loves. Francis D. Parkes. Orin. Betty. Judith. Sheila . . . The water flows in. We sink to the last level. Everything is moving, connecting, sliding, sinking . . .

We're through.

Looking back, the three levels are lit up like a carnival. There are no sounds. The lights in the Canal fade into one light. We drop the pilot. The breeze freshens. The rain has stopped. I crawled across the deck, dragging the bag. I managed to find my cabin before I passed out.

I'm not cold or warm. I might be approaching both. I don't remember when I've last fallen asleep. I'm not asleep or awake. I first met Meridith over a jar of artichoke hearts. But it's Lockett now . . . There's no possibility of an erection. The supermarket was crowded. The colors were warm. Lockett's hands moved easily over the frozen-meat packages, slipping them into his army overcoat. We discovered each other stealing. I had four jars of artichoke hearts in my pocket. Lockett kept me from being busted. He straightened me out. He sold me a doctor's bag and gave me connections.

I don't need to look around. The bag is in the center of the cabin. Sunlight streams through the porthole. There are loud voices outside and the grind of winches. I went to the porthole. The ship is being unloaded. It is very hot. We must be pulled up next to an island. I have been here before. I remember the pastel houses, the tin warehouses, the curve of the bay, the palm trees and oil refineries. I returned to bed. I have to leave. That much is clear. I have no memories. Except for Lockett. He's coming on. Nog has been canceled. He couldn't make it out of the park. He found no help and drowned himself in two feet of water.

There are hundreds of dollars in the bag. I can take a plane and carry the bag in myself. I found a razor and blade in the bag. I shaved. They might not recognize me. I looked in the bag again and found a pair of dark glasses. I put the dark glasses on and tucked my hair under the Stetson. I returned to the bunk. I've been around the Horn and the Cape of Good Hope. I'll return to the room over the river. Bridges will connect everything. I can put it together that way.

I'm out of the bed. I put one foot in front of the other until I reached the door. I touched the knob. But I still have the bag. What I should have done was get rid of the black bag, what I am beginning to remember was that I did get rid of the black bag. I put it under the bunk. I remember something like that. There was a black bag, although I know too that nothing happened and I haven't traveled around with the black bag. I touched the knob again. There was a quickness, certainly, as if I were about to be sure of something. But it's out of my depth to know what has happened, to touch a doorknob and make a report. I'm not up to that. There have been events, of a sort, and they have occurred quickly, one after the other. The Canal wasn't invented. I'm sure of that. And the rain was cool enough. That was several days ago. And there is Lockett now. I'm lighter. I haven't eaten. This day is lighter than the last. I barked. That's not true. I have to watch that. I don't need to bark against the sound of the winches. I returned to the bunk. There has been no decision except that I'm moving on. I have turned my back to the sea, for one thing, and am facing the island. I got up and grasped the bag, and my foot, as if by itself, took a step that was followed by the other foot, at last, and I was moving on, down the alleyway and gangplank and into a cab.

I flew to New York.

Irving Wallace

Author of THE PRIZE
and THE MAN

The Sunday Gentleman

Unforgettable true stories by one
of the most widely read novelists of our time

75185/75¢

If your bookseller does not have this title, you may
order it by sending retail price, plus 15¢ for mailing
and handling to: MAIL SERVICE DEPARTMENT,
POCKET BOOKS, A Division of Simon & Schuster,
Inc., 1 West 39th St., New York, N.Y. 10018. Not
responsible for orders containing cash. Please send
check or money order.

PUBLISHED BY
POCKET BOOKS

(A 3/9)

THE
PAINTED
BIRD

Jerzy Kosinski

95037/95¢

If your bookseller does not have this title, you may
order it by sending retail price, plus 15¢ for mailing
and handling to: MAIL SERVICE DEPARTMENT,
POCKET BOOKS, A Division of Simon & Schuster,
Inc., 1 West 39th St., New York, N.Y. 10018. Not
responsible for orders containing cash. Please send
check or money order.

PUBLISHED BY
POCKET BOOKS
(A 5/9)

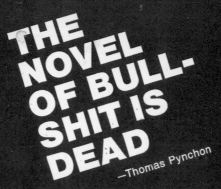

THE NOVEL OF BULL- SHIT IS DEAD

—Thomas Pynchon

"This strikes me as probably the most original, exciting and talented new novel since Thomas Pynchon's *V.*"

—Richard Poirier
Editor, *Partisan Review*

"This is an excellent book, full of unhealthy mental excitement."

—Donald Barthelme,
author of *Unspeakable Practices,
Unnatural Acts*

"It attempts, quite successfully, to reproduce in the reader's mind the simplification, the slight and continual dissociation from ordinary jagged reality...normally achieved by using soft drugs to tinker with the nervous system."

—*Atlantic Monthly*

"Something I'd like to have written!"

—Steve Lerner,
Village Voice

 PUBLISHED BY
POCKET BOOKS
PRINTED IN U.S.A.